ART
DAMAGED

ART DAMAGED
a novel

iUniverse books may be ordered through booksellers or by contacting:

iUniverse
1663 Liberty Drive
Bloomington, IN 47403
www.iuniverse.com
1-800-Authors (1-800-288-4677)

Because of the dynamic nature of the Internet, any Web addresses or links contained in this book may have changed since publication and may no longer be valid. This is a work of fiction. All of the characters, names, incidents, organizations, and dialogue in this novel are either the products of the author's imagination or are used fictitiously.

ISBN: 978-1-4401-6744-7 (pbk)
ISBN: 978-1-4401-6745-4 (ebk)
ISBN: 978-1-4401-6746-1 (cloth)

Printed in the United States of America

iUniverse rev. date: 9/16/2009

ART
DAMAGED

a novel
Nora Novak

iUniverse, Inc.
New York   Bloomington

Dedicated to my lovely mother,
Emmy Albertina Bogaerts-Leysen

Acknowledgments

I thank my mother for her unconditional love, enthusiasm, and support. I would like to thank my brother, Mark, for his inspiration and encouragement. Thanks to M. Lewis Stein for his editing, and a special thanks to B.R. Gilbert.

Contents

Live, Love, No Regrets

Her high heels clicked across the smooth, shiny cement as she walked swiftly to her desk. She was dressed in a classic black and white Chanel knock-off that she'd picked up in downtown LA, while on the prowl for her next work outfit. Nina adjusted her lacy slip that peeked out of her hemline and slid carefully into the high-backed swivel chair. She wondered how she had managed to sit at such a badly designed desk in the small contemporary art museum for ten years. It's not that she wasn't content with her position in the facility; the job had certainly fulfilled her on many levels. The perks weren't bad either. Her first few years at the museum were very exciting, with dynamic exhibits and glamorous fundraisers. She met famous artists and all of Orange County's glitterati alongside gallery owners, curators, artists, collectors and trendy art lovers. The museum's creative atmosphere had been instrumental in helping Nina rediscover her own talent as a mixed media artist. She quickly became a fixture in the local revitalized art community and her highly stylized paintings were often exhibited in group and solo shows. But what did anyone really know about her? Guarded about her past, the alluring, leggy blonde had tried hard to fit in. She soon adjusted to the sunny atmosphere that the museum provided and its embracing sense of belonging in that milieu. Nina enjoyed the camaraderie of some of her co-workers and looked forward to chatting with the docents and greeting the members and students. Happily ensconced at her desk, she could take a personal call and savor a cappuccino while breezing through the latest *Art in America.* All of that had recently changed, however, with a few key positions that had been newly filled. A dark, ominous cloud now loomed over her work days.

Nina glanced at her glittery Bulgari watch and realized it was almost noon. Just minutes until *freedom,* her lunch break. An incoming call on line one interrupted her musings.

"I'm expecting the Mortonsons for lunch. Direct them to the café and let them know I'm on my way," Amanda Keller ordered.

"Of course," replied Nina politely. Amanda, a new threat to Nina's position, was currently the new director at Emerald Bay Contemporary Museum of Art, also known as the EBC. She was an east-coast transplant, and the bone-thin redhead already had the staff whispering about her drinking problem and was making changes that would alter Nina's comfortable working situation. Amanda had recently teamed up with Helen Boyle, the snarky new director of visitors and relations who was Nina's new boss.

Helen, a big woman with a nasty disposition and a face like a clenched fist, had taken an immediate disliking to Nina, making life at the front desk unbearable. The combination of Amanda and Helen was lethal, and together they were wreaking havoc. Helen, an online dating junkie and blatant man-hungry woman, complained that her wimpy husband wasn't coming close to satisfying her insatiable appetite and was very excited to discover her new favorite site: xhornymen.com. Nina shuddered at the thought of it. She could hardly believe that this low-rent woman was now her new boss.

Nina dreaded the arrival of Helen and Amanda, but luckily it was almost lunchtime and she could get Angie to cover for her. Angie Kwan handled the sales and rental department and was Nina's best girlfriend and confidante. A slender girl with dark, velvety, almond-shaped eyes and long, glossy black hair, she looked like a young, Asian version of Elizabeth Hurley. Nina, originally from Luxembourg, had striking features, smoky green eyes, and an aristocratic profile. Nina felt that she and Angie both possessed a similar unusual beauty; it was a foreign-born kind of thing, they decided. The two girls hit it off right away and gossiped endlessly about the staff, giving them code names. Amanda Keller's was Killer, and Helen Boyle's was FT for fat tramp. They were very fitting, they thought.

"Hey, Angie, cover for me while I run out to lunch. Killer and FT are on the way."

"Yeah, okay, don't be gone long. Where are Justine and Nadia?"

"I haven't seen them all morning. They must be hanging out

3

in the storage room," replied Nina. Justine and Nadia, scrappy young lesbians with edgy haircuts and bad attitudes, had a thrift-shop, ghetto girl look, with random tattoos and piercings. The inseparable twosome ran the museum's gift store and had become Helen's personal pet girls who often snickered behind her back. They had recently discovered obscene e-mails Helen had sent at work to her new Internet guys and were just biding their time for promotions.

"Oh God, here comes Killer and FT," sighed Nina at the sight of the two women approaching the front desk. She swore the earth shook with Helen's every step. She moved like a rhinoceros in heat. Amanda, on the other hand, was at least visually tolerable, with her pencil-thin frame clad in all black Prada and Marc Jacob flats. Helen's look was *Beyond the Valley of Trailer Trash*. She had a tendency to pack her hefty torso into low-cut tops that accentuated her bulging midriff. She squeezed herself like a stuffed sausage into a pair of jeans that no woman her size should be wearing to work in a cultural establishment. Nina, on the other hand, had received many compliments on her appearance and demeanor and had been told that her presence added a much-needed shot of elegance and glamour to the museum's front reception. The sight of Helen lunging in pointy spike heels, waving a Virginia Slim in the air with her pinched face, was enough to make Nina lose her appetite, and she had so looked forward to lunch. To think that this mean-spirited hulk of a woman was taking over was hard to swallow. Helen had cleverly managed to hook up with and influence the new director,

Amanda, an alcoholic feminist fashionista from Manhattan. Oh, *quelle horreur!*

"Have the Mortonsons arrived?" asked Amanda.

"No, they haven't," replied Nina. "I'm off to lunch," she added, feigning a polite smile.

Helen heaved her chest over the desk. With smoky breath and a condescending tone, she asked, "Before you run off, did you know that your numbers are *down?*"

Numbers, ah yes, she knew very well what she meant by *her numbers.* Nina was in charge of admissions and attendance, which, in fact, were down. Never mind that the majority of the art-going population of Southern California couldn't even find the place. Was it her fault that the museum was built on a cliff overlooking the Pacific Ocean, concealed by an abundance of palm trees? Was it her fault that the only two-lane winding road leading to the museum was easily missed by even the savviest of travelers? The city simply wouldn't allow more signage. Those clever enough to find the turn often drove right past the tucked-away, nondescript building. The overhead banners promoting new exhibits were rarely noticed. What was she supposed to do? Run out to the Pacific Coast Highway and flag people down? Not a day went by without an aggravated customer remarking on how difficult it was to find the place. MapQuest's directions were extraneous and more confusing. The main exhibit was down for two weeks while the Warhol Retrospect was being installed, and everyone in town had already seen the current permanent collection. So … yes, the numbers were down. Did she have to be so nasty about it?

"I'm sure those numbers will shoot right back up when the Warhol show opens. Gotta run," she said, tossing her hair back as she darted off to the parking lot. "Thank God, fresh air," she said to herself, feeling relieved. "Bloomies, here I come."

***

Nina shimmied into her black metallic Mercedes C240 and snuggled into the soft grey lamb's wool seat that matched the pearl grey interior, perfumed with a leathery musk. God, she loved her car. Caressing the curve of the steering wheel, she kicked off her heels and sank her bare feet deliciously into the carpet. This was her sanctuary away from the front desk. A glamour girl needed a luxury car in this town; after all, you couldn't valet properly without one. Turning on her favorite radio station, 103.1, to catch Jonesy's Jukebox, she thought about all the Mercedes she'd owned over the years. Was this her fourth or fifth? She'd lost track. The first one was a cream-colored 290 SL with red leather interior that her father bought in Germany and had shipped to the States. There was a lot of mileage on that car before she got her hands on it. She drove it right into the ground, smashing into a freeway embankment late one very drug-addled night, but it was such a solid little tank, she still managed to get home in one piece.

That Mercedes was followed by a cherry-red 550SL sedan with camel-colored interior, an absolutely gorgeous car until it got showered by a stream of bullet holes. Leaving Jumbo's Clown Room one night, she made the mistake of attempting to scare off a group of young Hispanic vandals who taunted her when exiting the club. How was she supposed to know they were armed and dangerous? Bullets narrowly missed the back of her neck, and the entire rear window was shot out, which certainly took some explaining at the Beverly Hills Mercedes dealership.

But her favorite car was the gleaming silver C230 convertible that a short-lived but very generous sugar daddy gave her one Christmas. After foolishly loaning it to her neighbor, Rhoda, a fast-talking coke dealer whose main client was J. N. (a famous actor), she came very close to losing that one. Apparently Rhoda had taken a bootleg Quaalude to unwind before going out on deliveries. When she decided to stop for a quick bite at the farmer's market, she was pulled over for weaving out of the parking lot. The officer noticed a vial of coke on the front seat, and of course, she was arrested and the beautiful Mercedes was confiscated. It was an absolute nightmare getting the car back. And what did she get in turn for all her troubles? A badly stepped-on gram slid under her door with a pink post-it stuck on saying, "SORRY." Nina would have preferred an introduction to J. N. at the very least. Meanwhile, Rhoda's charges were dropped, her business thrived, and she bought a Mediterranean-style house in the Hollywood Hills.

"Ah, only in LA," Nina sighed.

***

The atmosphere in Bloomies felt crisp and clean, fragrant but not too heady. The 2004 spring season looked particularly colorful. There was such a dizzying array of gorgeous handbags. She really had her heart set on a new pink-and-white Christian

Dior bag but exercised great restraint to not purchase it, knowing she might be unemployed soon. Fighting the urge to whip out her Bloomies credit card, she suddenly eyed the new line of Murakami-designed Louis Vuitton bags she'd seen everyone sporting lately and remembered the first one she ever bought.

Living in the south of France one summer, she shared a bedroom with a blonde bisexual French girl named Chloe. The hotel was directly over a *patisserie*, from which wafted the delicious smell of croissants in the morning. The little room had no shower or toilet, just a sink and bidet, but they didn't care; they were young, beautiful, and very tan. While lying out on the beach in front of the Carlton Hotel, they met an exotic multilingual girl named Sascha, who made it her business to know every foreign high roller from Monte Carlo to the Palm Beach Casino and back. Sascha was always looking for new girls, especially blondes, to be seen around the tables while the men gambled. Nina spoke passable French and was something of a man magnet and flirtatious by nature, so hanging around high rollers seemed like a fairly easy and lucrative gig. The men gave Nina and Chloe stacks of chips, which they happily cashed right in. The girls made piles of money and laughed all the way to the nearest Louis Vuitton shop and bought complete sets of luggage! She could finally travel in style. The classic steamer trunk could easily hold all her big, beautiful size-ten shoes that she had been so awkwardly been lugging up and down the Cote D'Azur.

If only she'd had the good foresight to keep those fabulous French designer heels, she could have creatively incorporated them into some kind of mixed media art pieces … *art*. She suddenly realized that her lunch break was over and it was time to dash back to the museum.

***

As she wolfed down a handful of roasted almonds and a chicken breast she'd brown-bagged from home, Nina raced back to the car; she could not be late. The museum was now buzzing with activity as the installation crew darted in and out with a great air of authority. Thankfully, Killer and FT were nowhere in sight. The opening of the Warhol Retrospect was expected to be a blockbuster show, and it was only a few days away. Justine and Nadia were putting the newly arrived Warhol merchandise out on display; posters, pillows, calendars, clocks, mugs, T-shirts, and tote bags.

"Hey, Nina, check out these totally cool T-shirts," said Nadia. "Yeah, you're going to love this one," added Justine, handing her a size small with Little Joe (Joe Dellesandro) on the front.

"Oh my God," Nina squealed. "I've never seen this one before. Angie, get over here and try on these shirts with me." They grabbed the T-shirts and ran into the ladies room to try them on.

"They look so cute on," said Angie. "Let's go model for Rikki and Jessie." Rikki and Jessie were the museum's current punk-rock security guards, young, skinny art students, kind of Indie rocker types with a Ramones look. The EBC was unique in its succession of punk-rock guards. They came and went, some staying a few months or a few years, always referring their friends for the job, keeping it in the family, so to speak. They all looked similar and were somewhat interchangeable. Nina enjoyed working with her guards, sharing rock 'n' roll stories with the boys while poring over the latest *Mojo, Rolling Stone,* and *Spin,* magazines and listening to everything from Velvet Underground to Radiohead on slow weekends. Rikki and Jessie excelled in girl watching, seeming to possess x-ray vision; the lads were in constant high alert mode for hot chicks in the galleries. Nina strolled out and did her little catwalk turn and spin for Rikki and Jessie.

"Hey, man, didn't you say you went out with that dude?" asked Rikki, eyeing Joe's image.

"Well, sort of," Nina replied. She recalled meeting him in LA in the Miracle Mile district, and against her better judgment, she took him back to her apartment, knowing he had already had more than his share of women, men, and everything in between. He was still pretty irresistible. She'd had a crush on him from his Warhol films, and he certainly lived up to his image behind closed doors. She ran into him years later, and he gave her his card, which read: "70s Warhol Superstar. Will work for food." *Wonder what he looks like now?* she thought. She made a mental note to find that card.

"Hey, better take off those shirts," laughed Jessie. "The glimmer twins are on their way."

The glimmer twins, also known as the *gay amigos,* were actually the museum's chief curator, Monty, and his assistant, Tyler. They were good looking and very butch, with shiny, shaved heads and buff physiques. They generally favored Hugo Boss suits and always made a very impressive entrance.

Rikki and Jessie immediately got into guard position, stationed at opposite gallery entrances, snickering with their backs to the wall. They had heard the stories of Monty patting the asses of unsuspecting guards when given the opportunity.

"Well, well, well, what do we have here? Joe Dellesandro T-shirts. Oh, Tyler, we have to get these. They are fabulous."

"Oh yes, they are just *too fabulous*," chimed in Tyler. "Great gift idea too."

"Miss Nadia, darling, wrap up a dozen larges, *toute suite,* and sign them off to the curatorial department," ordered Monty. "And toss in a couple of catalogs."

"So, girls, where's our manly crew?" asked Monty, glancing at the security monitors at Nina's desk.

"Looks like the guys are in gallery three," she answered.

"Oooh, they're installing the 'Liz' series," purred Tyler.

"Excellent," remarked Monty.

"Carry on, girls, we're off to the galleries." Nina watched the two walk away with an air of purpose and vitality. She certainly admired Monty for organizing the Warhol Retrospect, which was considered quite a coup for a small museum. He was a dynamic speaker with such dramatic flair that his gallery tours were always well attended by board members, visionaries, docents, and staff. Although he had a nasty streak and was prone to sarcasm and cattiness, he brought in a lot of big donors and could do no wrong as far as the board of trustees was concerned.

"Okay, guys," Nina called out. "You can relax for now. Monty and Tyler should be occupied for awhile. It's time for my afternoon coffee. Has anyone seen James?"

"He's out front having a smoke," replied Jessie.

James Turner, her former superior, now chief of security, was an easygoing man with a twisted sense of humor. He had been with the museum since it first opened and knew all of its inner workings. A wise old hippie at heart, he was a strict vegetarian and played saxophone with a jazz band on the weekends. He rolled his own cigarettes right out of a Bugler tobacco pouch and drank more black coffee than she'd ever seen anyone consume. He remained calm, patient, always ready to lend an ear. A tall, trim man with narrow shoulders and a weathered face, he had a deep, warm voice that put everyone at ease. Nina and James shared a true camaraderie over the years, but thanks to Helen and Amanda that was probably all coming to an end.

Nina prepared a steaming cappuccino with extra espresso in the café kitchen, grabbed a chocolate biscotti, and strolled outside to join James. She watched him enjoy a deep drag from a freshly rolled cigarette, simultaneously inhaling the salty sea air. They sat quietly on the post-modernism benches under a rusting Mark Di Suvero sculpture, sipping their coffee, admiring the view.

Gazing at the ocean, they watched the big, white-capped waves roll in and out to shore. A couple of surfers in wetsuits stood next to their boards among a cluster of noisy sea gulls, a typical Emerald Beach postcard view.

"We have seen some beautiful sunsets out here, haven't we, James?"

"Yes, we certainly have."

"I think it was … Peter Alexander's Retrospective opening night. Remember that sunset? It was spectacular."

"That was one of my favorites. I want you to know that I'm hoping they don't let you go, Nina. It just won't be the same without you."

"I know, thanks to the *Helmanda* takeover," said Nina. "What if Rikki and Jessie get canned and you have to hire real guards? What then?" She laughed.

"I don't know, and I heard Angie may be on the way out too. No, it will never be the same. Well, Nina, *live, love, no regrets.* Is that still your motto?" asked James, laughing, referring to the tattoo on the back of her left shoulder. Nina and her ex-husband, Ian, had the matching tattoos done the night before they got married. The only difference was that his was intertwined with guitars and hers with hearts.

"Yeah, I was a lot younger then. It seems like a lifetime ago now."

It was hard to believe ten years had gone by. Had she really been sitting down that long? No wonder her butt didn't look as firm as it used to. She would definitely make it a priority to tone up right away. Time to break out the Carmen Electra aerobic striptease workout DVDs her boyfriend, Tommy, had given her and bust a move. Nina watched James whip out his rolling papers and roll up another cigarette, a skill she had never mastered back in the day when she kept a little jewelry box full of marijuana in her bedroom closet. She wondered how much it would cost today.

"James, look, they're bringing in the Chairman Mao's. I better get back to work." Inhaling a big gulp of sea air, she stood up and stretched, took one last look at the ocean, and returned to her desk.

***

"Call for you on line two, Nina. I think it's Barry," said Angie. Ahh, Barry Hamilton, a restaurant and food critic for *Gourmet* and *Bon Appetit* magazines. He was a true connoisseur. They had shared some fantastic dining experiences over the years. She admired his intelligence, sophistication, and passion for great food and wine. His resemblance to George Clooney didn't hurt either. They ventured to every new eatery from OC to San Francisco to LA and back.

Barry, an exceptional man, was always there for her; unfortunately, he was still very involved with his ex-wife and teenage daughter.

"Hi, Barry, how's your day?" she asked cheerily.

"Well, it's just brightened now that I'm talking to you. Listen, there's an exclusive champagne tasting coming up at the newly renovated D' Orso's. I guarantee you will love it," he said with his typical enthusiasm. He was right, she needed no persuasion there. That was an offer she could not refuse. She loved French champagne; there was nothing like a chilled bottle of Veuve Clicquot with a gourmet meal.

"Oooh, champagne tasting. Sounds wonderful, Barry. Count me in."

"Great, I'll call you with the details. Oh, by the way, has anyone told you that you are beautiful today?" he asked.

"No, actually no one has. Thank you, Barry." He was still enamored with her after all these years. He was supportive of all her creative endeavors; he was her man for all seasons.

***

Nina observed Justine and Nadia busily at work on the Warhol display, arranging the merchandise in a clever and original manner. Their fresh ideas were unlike anything she would have ever thought of. She admired how well they worked together and was fascinated by their unique street style sense of fashion.

"Love what you're doing with those *Electric Chair* clocks, girls," she called out. Nina felt surrounded by young, art damaged hipsters with degrees she didn't have. She had been so busy traveling and living her crazy life that she never got around to going back to school. She always looked great, though, no matter what. Didn't that count for something? And didn't anyone wonder how she managed to look so damn good on her EBC wages? It wasn't easy showing up every morning in a chic and fashionable outfit; it took some very dedicated and savvy shopping, done mainly on her lunch breaks.

She recalled the first day she arrived in a little white suit ordered out of a Victoria's Secret catalog, carrying a Coach handbag and a doctored-up resume that Barry put together for her. She strode into personnel and was hired on the spot. She was absolutely thrilled. After all, art was her first love, and to be working in an ocean-side contemporary art museum—well, it all *seemed* so perfect.

No Kids, No Pets, No Baggage

No one had ever really questioned her previous employment history. The only contact called by personnel was Barry, who, of course, gave her an excellent referral. In retrospect, she had a good, long run at the EBC, certainly a lot longer than any of her other jobs. The museum felt like home, and she simply wasn't ready to give up her position yet. But with Killer and FT on the rampage, it looked as though her sweet gig could sadly be coming to an end. Even more frightening, at forty-six, she was already older than most of the staff and had no backup plan. To be suddenly unemployed was frightening. She had certainly honed her job skills over the years and still had her looks, but she had to face the fact that Emerald Beach was teeming with young, bronzed, beautiful blondes. God *they were everywhere!*

In a league of her own, Nina managed to maintain a fresh and youthful attitude and was often complimented on her sleek and sexy appearance. Tommy, her new boyfriend, was considerably younger and didn't seem to be at all bothered by their age difference. He absolutely adored her and Nina was crazy about him too. Unfortunately, Tommy lacked an element of sophistication and level of success she was accustomed to in her men. She felt as though she was continually training him but was willing to overlook his shortcomings for now because he was so much fun and an absolute dead ringer for Clive Owen. She did a double take when she first saw him at the Emerald Beach Regency hotel bar, where he was working at the time, attracting a crowd with his bottle-tossing skills behind the bar. She shimmied right up front and gave him the most seductive glance she could muster, and they'd been dating ever since. Tommy was pretty irresistible, she had to admit. Everybody liked him. Besides Tommy and Barry, the other man in her life at the moment was Maximillian Habsburg, a very wealthy, suave older gentleman, an actual direct descendant of the Luxembourg Habsburg family. He reminded her of Christopher Plummer in *The Sound of Music*, but Nina was no Julie Andrews, and Maximillian was, as far as she knew, a semi-retired banker who *traveled an awful lot.*

Nina's friends were continually amazed at her ability to juggle men and their willingness to help support her lifestyle in various ways. She never experienced a man shortage, unlike most women in her age range. Since motherhood had completely eluded her, "No kids, no pets, no baggage" was her personal quote du jour. Her lifestyle had given her time to cultivate relationships with a few good men who were quite devoted to her. Lately, though,

Tommy complained that they didn't spend enough time together. She would have to do something about that, ASAP.

"Hey, Nina, snap out of it," said Angie. "It's time to go. I already closed up sales and rental and admissions!"

"Oh, right, let's get out of here." The girls quickly set the alarms and raced to their cars. Nina tore out of the parking lot like an Indy racecar driver, flipping up her pink and silver cell phone, and pressed nine on speed dial for Euro-Gourmet Drive-Thru. "Hi, this is Nina. I'd like to place an order for a salad Nicoise with extra dressing. Yes, for pickup please. Five minutes. Okay, thank you."

This was the only French drive-through in town that she knew of where she could get good fast food, especially after a tough day at the EBC. She used to love the place when it was first opened by a group of very fashionable French transplants. Recently, however, it had been taken over by some very curious young Brazilians, and she noticed the dishes tasted different every week. She tried communicating with them about it but was usually ignored, as they preferred to chatter rapidly in Portuguese among themselves. It occurred to Nina that the things she particularly liked in life were often discontinued. For a fleeting moment she imagined the Euro-Gourmet Drive-Thru might in fact be a cover for something else as she observed the continual lack of customer service and the ever-declining number of clients.

She pulled up to the takeout window, paid for her salad, and merged back onto the coast highway, enjoying the ocean view. *Too bad the coastline isn't more like Miami,* she thought. Now that would make life in Emerald Bay a lot more interesting.

Everything was pretty, new, and upscale but so conservative and generic. The buildings and the people all lacked *flavor*. Perhaps she was overdue for a trip to Europe or New York or at least a quick weekend jaunt to Vegas, anything for a change of scenery. Unfortunately, she could never get a weekend off from the museum, since she was locked into a Wednesday through Sunday schedule. But it looked like she might have plenty of time on her hands for travel soon enough.

***

She pulled into the cul-de-sac of her little Mediterranean townhouse. Entering her foyer, she kicked off her heels onto the polished marble floor. Grabbing the *LA Times*, she nestled into a plush, taupe-colored velvet sofa and ate her salad while reading the Calendar section. The living room resembled an opulent European salon with French antique armchairs, a Chinoiserie-style screen, beautiful Belgian rugs, and her prized possession, a brilliant eighteenth-century chandelier inherited from her grandmother. She loved her chic little abode and had Maximillian to thank for helping her purchase it; she couldn't have done it without him. She'd known him for over twenty years now. He was a friend of the family who still kept in touch with her mother. Nina looked lovingly at the bejeweled framed photos of her beautiful mother with her honey-blonde hair in a variety of up-do's, very Eva Gabor. She *always* wore a beautiful designer scarf to accessorize her outfits, her constant fashion trademark. Gracious and charming, she epitomized femininity and spoke five languages fluently. Nina realized she needed to be a lot more like her mother. She really missed her and would call her more often if it wasn't for that darn nine-hour European time difference.

Her father, on the other hand, was a different story. A tall, stern man with dark hair and eyes, he cut a striking figure. An Olympic swimmer in his youth, he had high hopes for Nina, training her like a Teutonic disciplinarian in every pool, lake, river, and ocean possible. Clearly, she was not cut out for the Olympics by any stretch of the imagination. Bathing caps and laps were not her idea of a good time. A talented artist, he was a successful painter known throughout the Benelux countries and taught her to draw. She had been surrounded by great art from birth; the gene pool was passed onto her, and as an only child, she spent many hours drawing and studying art history. Her parents had taken her to all the museums filled with work of the European masters. She particularly loved the Flemish fifteenth-century painters Campin and the Van Eycks.

It was never really clear to her why the Valliere family immigrated to Southern California when she was six years old. Somehow it remained a mystery. Her father worked for a small architectural firm and her mother stayed at home and was often homesick, missing the culture of her native Luxembourg. Nina found it difficult to fit in with the other kids with her refined manners and always felt different somehow. She hated the school's awful cafeteria food. Kids made fun of her accent, and she was astonished to find out that no one knew anything about Luxembourg and very little of European geography, history, or art. She was horrified that kids her own age didn't know a Matisse from a Rubens.

When her parents became citizens, the family returned to Europe for all their summer vacations and her father gave up the dream that Nina would ever become an Olympic swimmer. He became a very successful architect, establishing his own firm. With some minor college theater under her belt and big dreams of fame and fortune, Nina moved to Los Angeles to pursue acting and modeling. Distracted by relationships, summers in the South of France, a bad marriage, and too much partying, she lacked focus and never achieved the level of success she'd hoped for. Eventually her parents retired in Villefranche-sur-Mer so her father could return to his painting. After he died, her mother moved to Paris to be near her sister. Nina decided to change her lifestyle, moved to Emerald Beach, and got hired at the EBC. She thought about her mother every day and planned to ask Maximillian to fly her to Paris for her birthday this summer.

***

Nina walked over to her bookcase, which was bulging with art books of every possible art genre, from Byzantine art to abstract expressionism, surrealism, minimalism, Flemish masters, fauvism, neo-expressionism, post-modernism, and pop art. Lots of pop art. She ran her fingers slowly and sensually across the spines of each one: Rubens, Picasso, Matisse, Modigliani, De Kooning, Rothko, Pollock, and Warhol, a virtual sea of diverse and unending, beautiful art. She spent many evenings poring over these books for sheer pleasure and inspiration. The lower shelves were filled with biographies, novels, foreign-language dictionaries, and books on fashion and music.

The very last shelf was reserved for art catalogs she had been collecting from museums all over Europe, and of course, from every exhibit at the EBC. Most were signed by the artists, primarily southern California artists such as Tony De Lap, Peter Alexander, Larry Bell, Billy Al Bengston, Ed Moses, and Craig Kauffman.

***

Nina continued her way up the spiral staircase, gazing at all the paintings covering the walls. Her collection included a few by her father, some by emerging artist friends of hers, and many of her own mixed-media creations. At the top of the stairs was her favorite and most valuable piece, a large, sexy painting by British pop artist Allen Jones given to her by her ex-husband, Ian. The painting was the only thing he ever gave her during their brief marriage besides the emerald-cut diamond ring he put in her makeup bag the night before the wedding. She had reluctantly sold it after the divorce for a surprisingly large sum, never discovering how he had managed to acquire the ring or the painting. Things always tended to be somewhat sketchy and underhanded with Ian, which naturally drove her crazy.

She would always remember that fateful, sunny day when they first met outside the Byblos Hotel in St. Tropez where the Rolling Stones were staying while touring that summer. She was doing a photo shoot for *Oui* magazine, posing against a creamy white Bentley in a pale yellow Norma Kamali bikini. Looking like he just rolled out of the *Beggar's Banquet* cover, Ian stumbled out of the hotel and fixated on Nina's long legs and *that was it.* It was love and lust at first sight for both of them. A crazy and inexplicably mad chemistry hit the two of them, and they were immediately *inseparable.* Ian, a lanky, shaggy-haired, and unrefined but charming British rocker, had a killer wit and was a fairly talented guitar player but really had no visible means of support or any foreseeable future. As a verified Anglophile, Nina was a sucker for his accent and the fact that he could play all her favorite Stones songs on the guitar and do a spot-on Sean Connery impression. There was no denying that they were *in love.* After three passionately crazy days and nights in Ian's suite, culminating with matching tattoos, they flew to London with his bandmates, girlfriends and roadies in tow, and went straight to the magistrate's courthouse and got married.

Ian looked roguishly handsome in his all-white satin suit, no shirt, and snakeskin boots from Kings Road. Nina was resplendent in a slinky white bias-cut Halston halter dress and high-heeled white leather Charles Jourdan pumps.

They made a very charismatic couple around the London club scene, dazzling everyone with their good looks and charm so much that no one really noticed Ian's frequent swigging from a silver flask he kept in his jacket pocket and all the white powder he was shoveling up his nose. She was deliriously in love with him and had visions of being a glamorous, jet-setting rock star wife touring the world and living happily ever after in a decadently rambling British manor.

But alas, it was not meant to be. Ian's band, The Ian Blackmoor Experience, eventually got signed to a small, independent label and after months holed up in a tiny basement studio, they finally emerged totally strung out with a raw album that none of them were satisfied with. Their manager quit, sales were sluggish, and the records wound up in the discount bins at the local HMV. The bass player, Simon, the main songwriter of the band, overdosed on heroin, and the record label dropped them like a pair of satin hot pants.

Their only single "Take Her Down" never cracked the top forty, and after the advance money ran out, Nina and Ian wound up living in a drafty little flat on Marleybone High Street. Ian disappeared for days at a time. Desperately in need of quick cash, Nina started dancing at strip clubs in Soho to pay the rent. She found herself spending her afternoons combing the pubs for Ian, and would occasionally find him in The Cock and Bulls Balls in the East End. A boisterous pub known for catering to degenerate rockers and aging roadies, he could be found there playing darts and tossing back shots of Jack Daniels and pints of Guinness with his scrappy mates.

This was not the romantic rock star life that Nina had anticipated. She got tired of working the seedy Soho strip club circuit, the constant damp weather, and Ian's drugged-out, pub-crawling lifestyle. His wild rocker behavior and British humor that she once found so endearing no longer amused her. He begged her not to leave him, promising to change, but she knew he would drag her down. Tearfully, she divorced him and flew back to the United States.

***

The Allen Jones painting would always remind her of Ian,

and she wondered where he was now. Pausing dreamily in the doorway still thinking of the good times they once had, she entered her all-white and ivory Hollywood glam bedroom, dominated by a luxurious king-size bed. The upholstered headboard in tufted ivory leather and sumptuous, satin, diamond-patterned comforter with matching pillows had been designed for her in Paris. Flanked by mirrored art deco nightstands, it was, with the exception of a gleaming stripper pole, very reminiscent of *Dinner at Eight*. Complete with a Harlowesque chaise, creamy chenille throws, and plush white fur rugs, the bedroom was blissfully glamorous. It was her sexy hideaway from the rigors of the daily museum grind.

When her boyfriend Tommy, discovered that Nina had worked as an exotic dancer, he was so fired up that he immediately went to the nearest Platinum Poles-R-Us and purchased a shiny brass portable stripper pole and had it assembled and installed in a matter of minutes. He then rigged up a killer sound system wired in black lighting and rotating colored lights to flash on the walls and ceiling. Tommy was obviously a man of many talents. Now with the flick of a switch, day or night, her lovely deco bedroom could be turned into an instant mini strip club, much to the delight of both of them. Good times at *Chateau Valliere*.

Behind wide, double-glass doors, a vanity dressing area and bathroom beckoned with a pale marble sink and oversized bathtub surrounded by beveled-edge mirrors. Nina slipped into a fluffy white St. Regis bathrobe, lit a few vanilla candles, and started up a Gucci Rush scented bubble bath. Picking up the phone very seductively, she watched herself in the mirror and called Tommy.

"Hi, Tommy, how was your day?" she purred.

"Oh, hi, baby. How's my sexy girl? I was just thinking about you," he said, sounding aroused. "I sure miss you. What's my little sex kitten wearing?"

"Oooh, lots and lots of big, frothy bubbles," she replied breathily. "Tommy ... do you think you could ever learn to do a really good Sean Connery impression?"

"I could try, baby. What makes you ask that?" he asked quizzically.

"Oh, nothing really," she said softly. "I'll call you tomorrow. Sweet dreams."

Blame It on the Blonde

Back at her desk in full concierge mode, wearing a very fitted black Bebe suit that Barry had bought her, Nina was feeling well rested and ready to tackle any situation the day might have in store for her. Bring it on! With personable authority, she instructed the guards to open the big glass front doors for the morning's first busload. In poured teachers, docents, restless teenagers, and a few mothers who were accompanying the group. They were immediately divided into groups of ten by the docents while Nina did a quick headcount. One very worried-looking mom approached the front desk.

"Excuse me, miss," she asked gingerly. "I just wanted to make sure that there isn't anything, well, you know, offensive in the collections."

Offensive, thought Nina. *Is she kidding?* But this wasn't the first time she'd heard this kind of question, which usually came from the Christian elementary schoolteachers scouting out any possible nudity that might offend their precious kids. Nina could not understand this sort of Victorian mentality; with her European upbringing, their puritanical attitude was truly baffling. Apparently a field trip to Rome would have been out of the question for those kids. Following museum policy, she replied as politely and diplomatically as possible.

"No ma'am, nothing offensive here. Lots of impressionism and plein air paintings," that always seemed to calm them down, "in our permanent collection and work by very prestigious southern California artists. The installations and exhibitions galleries are closed down until the Warhol opening."

"Okay, thank you," the woman replied meekly and joined the groups. Did she really think these kids hadn't already seen nudity and every type of porn on the Internet? It seemed to her that a lot of parents didn't understand the beauty of art and that the least of their problems was whether their child viewed a nude painting or sculpture in a museum.

She noticed the bored-looking teens were getting antsy while the docents gave their talk on the museum's history. Meanwhile, Rikki and Jessie had cleverly positioned themselves to discreetly check out all the girls. This happened to be their favorite high school, known for particularly hot chicks frequently clad in halter tops and denim minis. Even James seemed more alert than usual with his third coffee refill in hand. He was happily married to a beautiful Indonesian woman, but like most men, he never passed up the available eye candy. The groups shuffled into the galleries, and suddenly Manuel and Jorge from maintenance, who were known to disappear mysteriously, often for hours at a time, suddenly appeared, following right behind, claiming the "Charles Ray" (a very lifelike piece) needed dusting. Nina hadn't realized that Emerald Del Mar's female students could generate that much interest among the male staff.

The senior citizens started to file in slowly, often driven in by vans from the local senior centers. They generally had lunch at the café after browsing through the gift shop and galleries, sometimes for hours.

"What kind of trees are those in the front, miss?" They were always asking about the trees and the flower arrangements on the front desk, which were often sent to Nina by Barry. A lot of the seniors were amateur plein air painters and former art teachers.

"Those are royal empress trees," she informed them happily even after the thousandth time, having a soft spot for the elderly. She had answered every question museum guests could possibly come up with and considered herself an invaluable source of information for the continual throngs of visitors who wanted to know everything. Where was John Wayne buried? Where can I get really fresh sushi? Students wanted help with their assignments on Michelangelo, even after she would explain to them that the EBC was in fact a contemporary art museum and directed them toward the Getty.

Nina gladly gave out dining tips to out-of-towners and locals alike, since that was her other area of expertise anyway. Many a guest actually returned for future visits, providing her with their personal reviews, and became members. She referred so many people to her favorite spots that she felt that these particular establishments should at least give her free cocktails and appetizers, and in fact, they often did. Well, if she lost her job, perhaps the Emerald Beach Visitors Bureau would hire her. Lately, the most frequently asked question at the front desk was not, "Do you know who you look like?" but "Where is the OC?" People actually came in looking for the TV show, as though Mischa Barton and the cast were filming down the road 24/7. Tourists hoping for celebrity sightings were very disappointed to find out the show was nowhere in sight. *The OC* was definitely putting Orange County on everyone's radar. It was now considered glamorous and no longer referred to as the Orange Curtain.

Nina continued to answer every question but furtively wished they would all just obediently file into the galleries, allowing her time to look at the new Dennis Hopper book, *A System of Moments*, that had arrived that morning in the gift shop. She continued to greet the public, answer the phones, and keep the guards in line. They had a tendency to migrate around the desk once the student tours were gone, much to the dismay of the administrative staff. She didn't feel like waiting for her lunch break and asked James to cover for her. She tore the seal off the book and quickly thumbed through it, and she did a double take about halfway through on a particular page. There was the image of a triptych, acrylic on canvas titled "Killer Pussy" with a poster of her girlfriend, Lucy LaMode, dressed as a teenage nurse and posing as the fifty-foot woman right in the lower center of the painting.

Lucy, the raven-haired lead singer of the '80s new wave rock band out of Phoenix called "Killer Pussy." They had a single called, "Teenage Enema Nurses in Bondage" that got a lot of publicity and radio play through KROQ. Nina had appeared in a number of shows in L.A and Phoenix, leaping out of cages brandishing a bullwhip to flocks of gay boys while Lucy sang "Teenage Nurses," "Pocket Pool," and "Bikini Wax." How in the hell did this wind up in Dennis Hopper's painting? She had to call Lucy immediately but was once again interrupted by those dreaded five words. "It's Helen on line one."

"Oh, shit, what does that woman want now?" she said, taking her sweet time picking up the phone. "Hello, Helen, what can I do for you today?"

"Don't mess with me, Blondie. I want to see you in my office *now!*"

"Why certainly, Helen, I'm on my way. Oh God, Angie, why can't that shrew leave me alone?"

Angie shot her a compassionate glance. "Good luck. James and I will keep our fingers crossed and hold down the fort." After checking her compact, Nina gathered her composure and headed toward the administrative offices in the connecting building. Passing the cold grey annex lobby, she continued down a long, fluorescent-lit hallway leading to a labyrinth of offices and cubicles desperately in need of renovation. Not feeling up to exchanging pleasantries with all of the education and curatorial assistants, she decided to simply acknowledge them with a smile and a quick hello on the way back.

Fortunately, Amanda was probably halfway to Berlin by now for a very important global museum conference, so she wouldn't run into her. The halls were permeated with the sweet, sickly smells of glazed donuts and See's candies. No wonder so many employees were gaining weight. Glued to their computer screens, they snacked listlessly while biding their time, hoping for pay increases and promotions. Passing by the coffee pots and powdered creamers and sugars at every station, she detected many wider asses than upon first arrival. She was thankful that her own ass had not spread even one centimeter over the past ten years. The atmosphere was positively claustrophobic; she already missed the museum's vast airiness and high ceilings. Suddenly she heard signs of life and elated laughter coming from Monty's office. Tyler and Monty were joyously rearranging their curatorial offices with new Phillipe Stark Queen Anne chairs.

"Oh Nina, sweetie, what are you doing over here? Look at our new chairs. Aren't they just too fabulous?" squealed Monty.

"Hi guys. Yes, they are absolutely fabulous. I've got to go, Helen is waiting for me."

"Oh you poor thing, she is such a bully. Would like to borrow a *strap on*?" Tyler asked. Monty and Tyler both howled with laughter.

"Thanks a lot. No more free guest passes for you two," quipped Nina. Leaving their offices, she bumped into and nearly knocked over the new human resources guy.

"Helen's really got it in for you, Nina. Let me know if you need some counseling afterward." Oh great, was the entire office aware of her predicament? She took a deep breath and knocked on Helen's door.

"Come in and have a seat," Helen ordered. "As you already know, your numbers are *down*, but that's not why I called you in here. A complaint has been made about you by one of our guests last weekend. Apparently you harassed one of our member's children and did not abide by our museum policy. I have dispensed memos to the executive director and all of the administrative staff regarding your inadequate customer service."

Nina bristled. "What? Are you kidding? You sent out memos to everyone before even bothering to talk to me and find out what happened?"

"I am *not* through. The customer is always right. I don't think you realize the gravity of this situation. I've started an official file on you, and it will be on your record permanently," said Helen gleefully. Trying to remain calm, Nina thought to herself, *What am I now, an art criminal with a growing rap sheet?* Nina paused and coolly studied Helen from head to toe, starting with the frizzy black hair, pinched face, and impossible body, right down to her gaudy shoes. She searched in vain to find some redeeming feature or quality to warrant this woman's place on the planet but she could find *nothing*. Sighing heavily, Nina said, "I've always followed museum policy, Helen. I think I've always maintained excellent customer service, and as you know, I personally greet about thirty thousand people a year under all kinds of conditions, such as finding the place, for starters! That *woman's kids* were running wild in the galleries. She refused to keep an eye on them and was shouting obscenities at the guards. So, if there is a questionable *situation* in the future, please speak to me about it before reprimanding me and sending out memos prematurely."

Helen reddened. "That's enough of your insolence. You need to study my updated training manual. I'm conducting a staff performance appraisal, and I will be watching your *every* move," she snapped. Nina bolted out the door in an agitated state. How much more could she take? FT was plotting her demise and would find any reason to get rid of her. If only Helen would get in her big bronze Suburban and drive off a cliff. After all, Emerald Beach was known for its thick marine layer. The coastline could get very foggy, causing bad visibility, and if someone *accidentally* tampered with her brakes, she could lose control of the vehicle and plunge right into the cold, dark Pacific Ocean. *Actually, that would be a good place for her,* thought Nina. Her mind raced with various plots, but none seemed feasible. She had seen way too many noir crime movies. There simply was no such thing as the *perfect* murder. Or was there? She walked swiftly back down the halls, now noticing a few unfamiliar faces. Apparently there had been quite a bit of turnover in recent months. She suddenly felt like such an outsider and was in no mood to make small talk with anyone. She could not get back to the museum fast enough. Still reeling, she attempted to settle in at her desk when there was another call from Helen.

"I just got an urgent call. I've got to run to LAX. I may not be back by the end of the day and there's a special events team coming I need you to deal with."

"Yeah, sure, I'll take care of it," said Nina. Why are you going to LAX? Anything wrong?"

"Well, I've got to attend to Amanda. She isn't, uhh, feeling well, and I have to get her on another flight."

"Amanda missed her flight to Berlin? How did she manage that? Never mind, just keep me posted." Justine and Nadia sauntered over, snickering like toxic twins having overheard the conversation.

"We know what happened to our Ms. Amanda Keller," Justine blurted. "She was knocking back vodka martinis at the airport bar and was too drunk to make it to the gate. Ha ha ha, she passed out right in the terminal."

"*What?* How did you know that?" asked Nina incredulously.

"We have our sources," Nadia retorted. They looked at each other, grinning. "Did you know that she had two DUIs in Connecticut? Why do you think Helen's always driving her skinny ass around town?" said Justine.

"Yes, actually, I did hear that one. Any more dirt?"

"We know that Helen put Amanda's pictures and profile up on xhorneymen.com without her knowing. Believe me, we have dirt on *everyone*. Hold on, new text coming in," giggled Nadia.

"All right you two, put your cell phones away, get back to work, and save some gossip for my coffee break." James strolled over from the galleries sipping his coffee and leaned over the desk.

"Did I miss anything? How did it go with Helen?"

"Clearly, the woman is working on my character assassination and plotting my early demise," Nina said, fanning the air. "Helen wants me eliminated. What can I do? Too bad you and I and Monty can't just run this place and bring in Gianni Murano, who would have been a great director."

Gianni was the husband of the previous director, Paula, now deceased. She was an upstanding, classy woman who ran the museum beautifully for years. Gianni was a passionate art collector and tremendous fundraiser and was much loved by the community, and after Paula died in a car accident, there was talk of bringing him on as the new director. Nina always thought Gianni was a very appealing man and considered calling him after the appropriate grieving time hoping he would take over Paula's position. Unfortunately, the East Coast Brigade, featuring Ms. Amanda Keller and her geeky media lounge squad, showed up to facilitate the EBC's new global mission with Helen worming her way right in, creating the present team in operation. It had been all downhill after that.

The Paula Years, as Nina referred to them fondly, were good years.

***

A group of docents sauntered up to the front desk, their oversized handbags in tow.

"Hi, Nina, can you hold our bags for us please? We are doing a preliminary Warhol walkthrough."

"Of course, ladies, let me know if you need anything." Nina enjoyed the docents; they were a friendly enough bunch of women and a few men. She had managed to remember most of their names and had many pleasant conversations about the exhibits and their personal lives. Many were former teachers, some divorced or retired. Several had wealthy husbands and had time for volunteer work. Most were well educated, well traveled, and definitely had a passion for art. One thing she noticed about the women, with a few exceptions, of course, was their idea of how mature women should look and dress. Perhaps it was their age-appropriate concerns, imposed by society, something that Nina, with her built-in sex appeal, didn't really adhere to. She could give the ladies a few tips and start an after-hours' workshop. "How to increase your sex appeal, keep your *man or men* happy, and enjoy art all at the same time!" She could even invite them over for pole-dancing classes. After all, it was the current craze sweeping OC from young professionals to soccer moms. That would be fun, thought Nina, but probably not in her best interest with her upcoming staff performance appraisal. Too bad, because Helen could benefit from it as well. On second thought, only an *extreme makeover* could help her.

Eager for a change of atmosphere, Nina decided it was high time to take a break and go shopping. Whipping a power bar out of her red leather Michael Kors bag, she zipped over to sales and rental. "C'mon Miss Angie, let's take a break and hit the mall."

"We can't leave now. What about Helen?" inquired the ever-sensible Angie.

"The old FT won't be back for hours. In fact, she probably won't be back before the end of the day. It's really slow right now, and there's a big sale at Bloomies that we do not want to miss."

"What do we need there that we can't live without?"

"We need new outfits for the Warhol opening, little sister. We're running out of shopping time and we have to look fabulous. This may be our last big EBC bash."

"Maybe you're right, let's go," Angie agreed. They rushed over to Bloomies and breezed inside like a pair of fashion divas, scanning the racks with veteran aplomb. Accustomed to shopping in a hurry, Nina had developed a very quick and discerning eye for picking out the right clothes. She immediately spotted a silver and crystal embellished metallic Gucci mini dress.

"I just found the perfect dress for you, Angie. This will be stunning with your long black hair and long legs. This is *the one*."

"It's gorgeous. Oh my God, are you crazy? Look at the price tag!" screeched Angie.

"So what? It's half off the original price, and it's a Gucci! You have to get it," Nina insisted. "Look, you can always tape in the tags and return it later to another Bloomies."

"Do you still do that? You are such a bad influence. Okay, I'll try it on. Now, let's find you a dress. Mmmm, what about this slinky white BCBG number?"

"Very pretty. Oooh, wait a minute, I think I found it. Take a look at this yummy black silk jersey Vivienne Westwood. It's so chic and sexy." The girls headed for the dressing rooms beaming with excitement.

"Ohmigod, Nina, you were right. This dress looks amazing! How are you doing?"

Nina finished zipping up the slinky black dress and admired herself in the three-way mirror from every angle. It fit like a *glove*. What a find.

"Are you ready, Angie? I'm coming out." The two girls strode out of the dressing room at the same time like models ready for the LA spring collection.

"Angie, you look fantastic."

"You do too. I love that dress. It's beautiful."

"I love it too. I feel like Heidi Klum!"

"It doesn't get any better than that," said Angie, giddy with laughter. "I'm afraid to ask. How much is it?"

"I am not even going to tell you. I'm just going to go ahead and put it on my American Express card, rack up some mileage, and give Maximillian a call in the morning."

The Best Is Yet to Come

Brandon White, the former chief preparator and now director of operations, had worked his way up the ladder at the EBC and was well respected by the staff and board of directors. An excellent craftsman, he was admired for his expert carpentry and inventive installations. He was a good-looking man, sandy haired, tall, and well-built, and he oozed an exaggerated sense of cool. He knew everyone in the LA and OC art scene, owned a small, hip gallery, and had included Nina's work in two group shows. As Nina watched him direct his motley, baggy-jeaned crew carrying in a giant Marilyn Monroe diptych into the galleries, she called out to him.

"Hey, Brandon, what's new?"

"Did you get my e-mail?" he asked. "We need to close up the permanent collection galleries tomorrow. The Warhol Retrospect is going to fill up the entire museum. Put up a sign to let people know that only the café will be open."

"Okay, will do. I better make a round and look at all my favorite pieces before they wind up in storage indefinitely."

Brandon walked over in his typical relaxed manner and asked, "So, Nina, any new talent in the gift shop?" She knew what he meant; Brandon definitely had an eye for the ladies and had no trouble getting them.

"No new talent here. We could actually use some help in the store. This place will be swamped once the show opens, but Helen won't hire anyone."

"Just between you and me, I can't stand the sight of her. She doesn't belong here," he snarled.

James strolled over. "Hey, Brandon, everything's looking good. Nina, there are some catering people waiting for Helen in the café."

"I was wondering when they were going to show up. I'll take care of those party handlers. Helen's probably still on the 405 in a manic mood chatting up her new online guys like a female trucker."

Greeting the catering team like she owned the place, Nina gave them the grand tour, reviewing the menu, setups, and various party arrangements, estimating the attendance and amount of food needed. The Emerald Beach crowd was a hungry one. She recalled one particular opening when everything was devoured within a half hour. The appetizers and buffet vanished, and it turned into a very disgruntled art-going mob. No one wanted a repeat of that scenario. Spectacular Catering was the best in OC, and they assured her that there would be an abundance of everything. Nina was working up an appetite and ready to call her fellow foodie, Barry, when she was interrupted once again by those frequent and aggravating words. "Helen's on line one."

"Hi, Helen, what's the update?"

"I'm stuck on the fucking 405. As for the update, I'll have you know that I've saved the day. I got Amanda on the plane, and she'll be back in time for the opening. Have you dealt with the caterers yet?"

"Yes, everything's fine," replied Nina.

"Good, because I won't make it back before closing and I have a very *hot* date tonight. I will deal with you tomorrow after the staff meeting."

"Yeah, okay. So, where is your hot date taking you for dinner?"

"Dinner? What dinner? Xhornymen.commers don't take you out for expensive dinners like your guys, miss glamour puss. I go straight to their place and make a meal out of them," she said, slurping and cackling uncontrollably.

"Sorry I asked. I'll see you tomorrow." Nina hung up, disgusted. The brief conversation left a bad taste in her mouth and a dark cloud over her head. She despised Helen but couldn't help but wonder why she was so fearless with these strange and horny men especially after the alleged date rape she'd cried about only a few weeks ago. Helen had called Nina, claiming she'd been date raped by one of her new guys, which was very hard to believe, considering no man needed GHB to get her in the sack. She asked Nina to cover for her and keep it quiet. Was Helen trying to get her sympathy? She was definitely sending her mixed signals.

***

Nina was in serious need of a nice glass of red wine; it was definitely time to give Barry a call for happy hour. "Hi, Barry, will you meet me at Dino's for cocktails?" she asked seductively. Dino's was an old school Rat-Pack themed restaurant on the waterfront with red leather booths and an outdoor smoking lounge. It had formerly attracted a mature crowd, but it was now inhabited by trendy young hipsters, rockabilly types and Betty Paige look-alikes favoring Sinatra music and cheap martinis. When she arrived Barry was already seated in their favorite corner booth, having ordered a bottle of Chateau Ferriere Marguax.

"It's so good to see you, Barry. You are looking so handsome," she said playfully while sensually sliding in next to him.

"And you are looking very beautiful as always."

"Thank you, but I'm certainly not feeling beautiful. Helen has me so stressed out. I think it's taking a toll on my looks. That woman is really cramping my style."

"We can't have that. Listen maybe you should go to human resources and complain about her," Barry suggested.

"No, he's a new guy. He doesn't have any clout. I'm afraid Helen's the shot caller now. I'm just going to have to hang in there and get through this somehow."

"That's my girl. You'll come out on top, don't worry," said

Barry with a glint in his eye as he scooted in closer to her. "So, when is your *Emerald Coast* magazine feature coming out? That's something for you to look forward to; I can't wait to see it."

She had recently posed for a four-page spread featuring art and fashion in a local glossy OC publication. Looking for a local, female artist who could also model for an upcoming spring issue, Jack Kowski, head of public relations and marketing at the museum, had suggested Nina to the publishers, and she wound up posing and leaping her way through Emerald Beach in a number of fabulous designer outfits. The feature was also supposed to include a bio and a few images of her paintings.

"You know, I'm not sure when it hits the stands, but I'm very excited to see how it turns out. I only got to see a few Polaroids the day of the shoot. Oh, by the way, I just finished the Rat Pack painting I made for you. It turned out great. I know you're going to love it. I think I'll title it *Ocean's Eleven*."

"Excellent. I have the perfect spot for it in my office," he responded.

"You are coming to the opening Saturday night, aren't you?"

"No, I'm so sorry, Nina, I can't make it. You know I would love to, but I'll be in San Francisco this weekend reviewing a new restaurant for *Bon Appetit* and *Wine Spectator*. Of course, I will be thinking about you. So tell me, what are you going to wear?"

"Oh, Barry, I just found a really beautiful dress today. I'll wear it next time we go out."

"I'm looking forward to it, so be sure to take lots of pictures and e-mail them to me. By the way, I freshened up your Spa Luxe card so you can get all the beauty treatments you need. Can't have my princess stressed out."

"Thank you so much, Barry," she said and kissed him sweetly. They finished their wine and watched the sunset to the tune of Sinatra's, "The Best Is Yet to Come."

Beauty in Bondage

Nina was almost home when she realized she'd left her little black leather Chanel day runner at the front desk. She did *not* like the idea of maintenance or the crew having a look at it even though it was unlikely anyone would be interested in her personal journal, but it was loaded with very private stuff, and with all the gossip floating around, *no one* could be trusted. So she decided to run back and get it.

As she approached the front desk, she noticed a big stack of magazines and videos. As she got a closer look at them, she saw the titles: *Sluts in Bondage*, *Bound and Gagged*, *Fetish Dolls*; what the hell? These had to belong to Brandon; she was aware of his kinky side. When she first arrived at the EBC from LA he approached her with an assortment of fetish catalogs, hoping she would model bondage gear for him. The S&M scene didn't really appeal to her; she'd worn her share of leather, latex, and rubber and dabbled in dominance at the infamous "Chateau M" in the valley and had more than satisfied her curiosity. The floor-to-ceiling sado-masochistic instruments and rooms with names like "The Inquisition" and "Depravation Chamber" that contained medieval-looking equipment didn't do it for her, nor did the wheelchair-bound help, sullen dominatrixes, and listless submissives. It was all very fascinating, but the dungeon life was simply not her style.

She heard the sounds of Danzig's "She Rides" coming from the back of the museum, so she ventured quietly through the galleries toward the loading dock support room, carefully unlocked the door, and stopped, aghast at the scene before her. Dressed like a Marquis de Sade of the art damaged underworld, there was Brandon aggressively flogging a young, masked, naked girl hanging from a beam. They were surrounded by restraints and shackles on the work benches, and whips and paddles littered the floor.

"Oh, my God!" Nina cried.

"What the fuck are you doing here?" he asked, peeling off his black leather hood to reveal beads of sweat running down his forehead.

"I forgot my day runner. I, uhh, saw the bondage magazines and heard music and I, I, uh … had no idea," she stammered. "Who is that blindfolded and bewigged little wench you've got hanging from the rafters, for God's sake?" Brandon removed the gag from the girl's mouth.

"Who is it, who's there?" the young girl asked, panic stricken. "You promised me no one would come in here."

Recognizing the squeaky little voice, Nina gasped, "Jesus, Brandon, that's the registrar's new assistant!"

"Listen, Nina, just calm the fuck down. You realize we have to keep this quiet. It can't leave this room, understand?" Unconvinced, she stared blankly at him.

"I don't know. You shouldn't be doing this here," she finally said, shaking her head.

"C'mon Nina, I'm sure we can work something out," Brandon pleaded.

"Okay, I'm listening."

"You know, some friends of mine are opening a new gallery in Venice, and I think your paintings would be a very good fit there. I could make sure you get in the inaugural group show opening."

"Oh really? Hmmm, I do like the sound of that. This little ritual of yours is a onetime thing, right?"

" No, actually I plan to be here every week because after I'm done with this session you so unexpectedly interrupted, I'll be making a mold of her torso and bust for a series I'm working on. I plan to exhibit my show in New York in the fall."

"How long has this been going on?"

"What difference does it make? You can't tell *anyone*. Not James, not even Angie. I have to complete my work. Look, I have an *in* with one of the art critics at *Art in America,* and I'm sure she can get you a nice review."

"I see. I didn't know you were a budding sculptor, and I'm certainly not one to stand in the way of, uhh, great art ... so all right. Your secret is safe with me. Carry on and I'll be on my merry way. *Please* throw a robe on that girl."

Eying a beautiful unfinished cabinet on the way out, she knew that everyone would assume Brandon was working on it after hours and would never suspect what he was really up to. Clever cover, she thought. Still, it was pretty risky considering James and the guards had all the keys and alarm codes and he would lose his job if this leaked. After grabbing her day runner and a bondage magazine, she dashed out and ran into Rikki and Jessie hanging out in the parking lot.

"Hey, what are you guys doing out here?"

"We have to work late for an architectural seminar in the auditorium," said Rikki.

"You guys don't need to go in the museum, do you?" asked Nina nervously.

"No, we're gonna lock up the offices, fill out our time sheets, and go. We heard FT called you into her office this morning. What happened?"

"Some bullshit about a complaint," said Nina, shaking her head. "Remember that skinny blonde woman with the two bratty, out-of-control boys?"

"Yeah, that psycho lady called me and Jessie apes! Can you believe that? We were just doing our job. Those little fuckers were all over the art."

"I know, she was really rude to me, and then apparently she stormed over to administration and filed an *official* complaint against me. Helen didn't bother to ask me what happened. She automatically blamed me for the incident. I'm sure she was thrilled to have something against me, and she immediately sent out memos to the staff."

"That sucks. Fuck her. Just forget about it. There are some nice gift bags in the front office. You want one?"

"No, thanks, I just want to go home."

"Hey what's that magazine?" Rikki asked.

"It's, uh, nothing you'd like. By the way, you still have my copy of *Performance.*"

"And you still have my Henry Rollins book. Bring it back tomorrow, and don't forget my Joy Division CD," said Jessie. "I'll burn a copy for you."

"Thanks. I've got to run. See you guys tomorrow." Thank God they didn't go in the museum and catch Marquis de Brandon and the intern in action. She would have loved a picture of that little scene; Nina usually never left the house without a camera, always keeping one in her handbag just in case. Unlike some museums, the EBC's policy was absolutely no photography in the galleries, but in order to accumulate her own personal documentation, she would go in early on Sunday mornings and photograph her favorite pieces from each new exhibit. She and the guards also took pictures of each other and had compiled some very tasty shots for their personal scrapbooks. Nina tried to shake the image of Brandon and the registrars assistant, and she hoped the poor girl wasn't getting any welts. On a brighter note, she would get her work in a cool new gallery in Venice and a guaranteed review in *Art in America*! All in a day's work! Now she could finally go home, put on the new Coldplay CD, and order in; or better yet, order Tommy in.

Art Barbie

Early the next morning, Nina, in a playful mood, picked up the phone. "Good morning, Maximillian, you handsome man It's your favorite leggy blonde calling,"

"Nina, darling, my lovely Nordic princess, it's so good to hear your sexy voice. How are you?"

"I'm fine, Max. I miss you; I never get to see you anymore. It seems like you are *always* traveling."

"I miss you too. What's new with you and your little museum?" he asked.

"*My* little museum is having a very big Warhol opening reception this weekend. I hope you can make it.

"I would love to, darling, I'm sure it will be fabulous, but I am leaving tomorrow morning. I may be gone for a few weeks. What is my beauty going to wear?" Nina loved how the men in her life were so interested in her wardrobe.

Coyly, she replied, "You know it's important that I look my best, and I found this absolutely heavenly Vivienne Westwood dress at Bloomies today that would be perfect. But it's, you know, it's just a teensie bit out of my price range, and umm."

He cut her off, "Consider it done, Nina, my love, you must get it. I will make a direct deposit into your account right after we hang up."

"Oh, Maximillian, thank you. *I love you.*"

"I suppose you will need a new pair of shoes to go with the dress to show off those sexy ankles."

"Actually, I did notice some Jimmy Choos that would be perfect."

"Yes, of course, get the shoes. I will expect a private fashion show when I return, and I will have a bottle of Cristal waiting for you with your name on it."

"That sounds wonderful, I can't wait. Call me from Vienna. Kisses, ciao." Nina loved those direct deposits; Maximillian had all her bank account information since he helped her get the townhouse. Feeling flush about the fat deposit, she dashed off to work, prepared to breeze through the staff meeting and take on the old FT.

As James and Nina filed into the community room, the rest of the staff were already milling about with their bagels and cream cheese, drinking coffee and orange juice in Styrofoam cups. Engaged in idle morning chatter, they were all trying to decide where to sit at the long conference table, as the seating arrangement could be crucial. Nina and James opted for the back end near the doors for an easier, and hopefully early, getaway.

Brandon sauntered in, Starbucks coffee in hand, and exchanged a knowing glance with Nina. Thankfully, there was no sign of his little S&M cohort. No one looked particularly happy to be there, but everyone got seated eventually and waited for the morning's agenda to begin.

In swept Helen like a red alert tidal wave at the Wedge. She suddenly seemed larger than life as she sucked the air right out of the room. The entire atmosphere shifted as she started the meeting with her brassy voice. She wore a dark green dress that was way too small for her bulky frame. Nina wondered if Helen even owned a full-length mirror or if she ever bothered to check herself out from the back. While Helen carried on about the importance of increasing membership and making this Warhol show the biggest blockbuster in the history of the EBC, Nina looked around the room and noticed everyone staring at Helen's mouth. Something was different about her lips. They were *huge*. Oh my God, she had her lips done. She suddenly looked like a big green blowfish. Stifling laughter, Nina elbowed James, making a fish face.

Helen finally stopped barking and let the staff get on with their reports and set the next meeting date. James slipped out the door with Nina right behind him, thinking she'd made a smooth getaway, but Helen grabbed her by the arm.

"Not so fast, *Art Barbie*, I want you in my office."

"But I've got a group of Visionaries on the way."

"They will manage without you for a few minutes; I've got something to show you." Reluctantly, Nina stepped into her office, which reeked of burritos and strong perfume. Nina noticed the crumpled-up Del Taco bags in the waste can and started to feel a little ill. As Nina eyed a jumbo coke on Helen's desk, she fantasized slipping some sort of undetectable poison into the dark liquid that would move swiftly through Helen's bloodstream when she heard, "Nina, I'm talking to you."

"Okay, Helen, what is it?"

"Come over here and look at my computer screen. Get a load of this. It's my favorite new site, that I discovered last night." Her voice rose with excitement. "Wellhungnready.com. I *love* it! Look at all these men. I'm in ecstasy!

Nina blanched. "My God, Helen, what is it with you? One minute you're chewing me out and the next minute you want to share your favorite X-rated site! Is this what you called me in here for?"

"Take it easy. Don't forget, I'm calling the shots around here now."

"Yes, well, that may be so, but you told everyone not to go online for personal use. I just don't feel comfortable looking at a bunch of naked men with you in your office."

"Don't give me that crap. Quit being such a prude and take a look at Randy4U. Isn't he awesome? I had my lips done this morning on the way to work just for him. We have a date tonight. How do you like my lips. Think they're *big* enough?"

"Uhh, yes … they are *definitely* big enough."

"I can't wait to wrap these new babies around Randy's big throbbing cock—"

"Stop, Helen, please." Nina was starting to feel queasy from the burrito smell. "I really don't want to hear the details."

"What is your problem, *Miss Nina?* Don't you think I've seen the way men look at you? I've heard all about the swanky dinners and the shopping sprees, and who the hell is sending all those roses to the front desk? How come no one is sending me any flowers? I have had it with you and your classy little mantrap. Just exactly what are doing to these guys? What is your *secret?* I want to know right fucking now."

"I don't have any secrets to share with you, Helen," Nina retorted with gritted teeth. "I need to get back to work," she said, grabbing the doorknob for support to make her exit.

"Oh that's right, go run back to your precious desk. You better get my new POS system mastered by the end of the day or I'll have your pretty little blonde head on the chopping block, *comprende?*"

Feeling ill and ready to heave, Nina ran all the way to sales and rental. "Oh my God, Angie, I think I'm going to be sick. I thought I could handle it, but I can't take anymore of her harassment. I need a break from that evil woman."

"Calm down, don't let that FT get to you. You've got to get a grip. She's jealous of you. Can't you see that?"

"I know you're probably right, but I think Helen has a split personality. She chews me out and then expects me to be her confidante. I can't take it, she's relentless. I can't stand being in the same room with her. Have you been in her office lately? It reeks of old burritos. Oh God, where are the Visionaries?"

"Monty's talking to them right now. It's okay, everything's under control," Angie said, reassuring her.

As the women began to filter into the gift shop, Nina settled down and focused her attention on the tight, swept back faces, flawlessly applied makeup, and freshly highlighted, well-coiffed hairdos. Dressed in St. John suits with coordinating accessories and big diamond rings, they exuded an air of wealth and stature, all appearing to be of an indeterminate age. She could spot the early facelifts all the way from the parking lot and taught Angie how to recognize them too, something she'd never really paid attention to prior to knowing Nina. The newer facelifts were harder to detect. All the fillers and injectables made them look a lot more natural. Emerald Beach was now one of the capitals of cosmetic surgery, giving Beverly Hills some stiff competition. Nina found these women fascinating, and she wondered what it would like to live a day in their life.

"Check out Mrs. Turnbull's face," Nina whispered. "It's so shiny it's blinding me. Must be freshly lasered. Looks like she had another brow lift too. I don't think she can even close her eyes all the way shut."

"I heard she had a botched Botox job and now she can't even move her forehead," Angie chimed in.

"Well, now that you mention it, I don't think her forehead's moved since that art auction fundraiser she hosted at the Emerald Bay resort last summer."

"She's on her third facelift and still managed to snag another husband," Angie announced. "I heard he's one of the top ten wealthiest men in SoCal."

"Wow, how do they do it, Angie? How do those women land Fortune 500 CEOs? I'm guessing they never date *bartenders*. You know they certainly didn't meet them at the Barracuda Bar," said Nina.

"You should appreciate Tommy more," Angie advised. "He may not be rich, but you would never be happy with one of those guys. Oh, here she comes. Hi, Mrs. Turnbull."

"Hello, girls, nice to see you. Are you ready for the big opening?"

"Yes, we are. Did you enjoy Monty's talk?" Nina asked.

"Yes I did. Monty is absolutely brilliant. I just adore that man. Well, girls, I'm meeting my husband for cocktails at the Ritz. Take care." Another Visionary, Christina Horchow, a petite woman with porcelain skin, fine features, and jet black hair, approached the display cases. She and her husband, Hank, were founders and corporate partners of the EBC, and their names were prominently displayed on the donor wall. The Horchows were well known for making very generous donations to underwrite exhibitions and frequently appeared in all the local social columns. Hank, an older-looking version of Donald Trump, was a big-time developer and had made a killing in real estate. He discovered Christina at Escada at the South Coast Plaza working as a sales associate while he was shopping for a dress for his first wife. Together, they personified the OC power couple. Christina arrived in spectacular gowns at all the black-tie charity events, and their extravagant cocktail parties were legendary. Clad in an elegant black Chanel pants suit, she was a tour de force of erasure. Not one line, shadow, or wrinkle marred her ageless and slightly frozen appearance.

"Hello, Christina, is there anything I can show you?" Nina asked.

"I need some gifts for a couple that collects Frank Lloyd Wright. Let me see the cufflinks, the clock and that scarf, the pens, and oh, the light screen reproduction. They'll love that."

Nina carefully pulled out all the items onto the glass countertop, remembering the buffet luncheon that Christina and Hank had last fall. They invited the entire EBC staff over for a special viewing of their new three-level home during its development stages. The couple had recently purchased four immense lots in Emerald Bay Terrace overlooking the ocean. Apparently, they were eager to share this with the commoners. The staff was treated to a brief speech by Hank in order to fully appreciate the unveiling of a large encased model of their future compound, followed by a tour of the grounds, including a very impressive glass elevator, which was built simply to take up the dry cleaning.

In spite of the chilly weather, a light buffet was set up al fresco so as to fully admire the spectacular view. To Nina's horror, only *plastic* cutlery was provided, once again showing that money doesn't necessarily equate class. On the way out everyone politely thanked the Horchows for a lovely afternoon. Knowing she would most likely not be invited back for the big party they would inevitably throw to celebrate the completion of their grand estate made her feel somewhat like a second-class citizen. She would have, however, gladly gone just to see Christina's bedroom closet, designed to take up an entire wing.

"I'll take all of these and a couple of Frank Lloyd Wright catalogs," said Christina.

"Sure, let me get Justine and Nadia to wrap these up for you." Where were those girls? They were never around when she really needed them. Then she spotted them sneaking out of the stockroom.

"What were you two doing in there? I need your help in the gift shop," Nina said curtly.

"We're busy working on a statement for an upcoming art installation that we're collaborating on for the Brewery downtown LA," explained Nadia.

"Do you have to work on that *now*?"

"Yeah, we do. The deadline for submission is tonight, and we've been so busy here with all the Warholmania that we didn't have time to finish it. Don't you want to know what we came up with so far?" asked Justine.

"Okay, hurry up, tell me. What's the concept?"

"We're thinking about having vagina-shaped balloons floating in an all-pink room with feminist slogans painted across the walls in black text to explore gender issues and promote female empowerment."

"I don't know, it sounds like Gloria Steinem meets Warhol meets Barbara Kruger to me. Needs some work, girls. Right now I've got Mrs. Horchow waiting in the gift shop to buy a bunch of Frank Lloyd Wright stuff, and we need the sales to keep Helen off our backs. So please get over there and take care of business."

"Yeah, all right, just chill, we've got it covered. Hi, Mrs. Horchow, how are you today?" Justine greeted her as they came into the gift shop.

"Hi girls, I'm fine," she said, giving Nina a disapproving look indicating that she didn't at all care for their appearance. "I just let Monty know that Hank and I will be having another luncheon, so all of you can enjoy phase two of the development before our final home completion. It's been such an exciting project we wanted to share it with the staff."

"Yes, it's *very exciting*. Unfortunately, for me, there is a possibility that I may no longer be working here," Nina revealed. "It seems that Helen may be bringing in her own interns and students."

"Really? I haven't heard anything about that," Mrs. Horchow said, trying to raise her eyebrows. "You've been here so long and we certainly need your *special* brand of glamour at the front desk. Maybe I should have a word with Amanda about Helen's plans. You know, Hank and I just adore Amanda. She's so cutting edge, really brilliant."

"Yes, she is brilliant, all right, when she's sober," Nina muttered quietly.

"What's that, dear?" Christina asked.

"Oh, nothing."

"Well, Nina, just have the girls take my packages to Brandon's office."

"Brandon's office?" she asked, surprised

"He's delivering a Richard Diebenkorn we just purchased to our Lhana Beach residence this evening."

"How interesting. I will see to it personally."

"Thanks, my driver is waiting for me. I have a fitting at Dior for my dress at the Warhol opening."

"I can't wait to see it. Bye." Nina said enviously, wondering if she would ever get to own or even wear a Dior gown. She better have a word with Brandon to find out if he was up to anything scandalous. Suddenly she visualized Christina in a dominatrix outfit and that bad comb-over toupee wearing husband of hers as a dog collared wearing submissive. Maybe he was more of a voyeur type and just liked to watch. She imagined them as a kinky S&M couple by night.

"Hey, girls how are you coming along with those packages?" Nina inquired, coming out of her salacious reverie.

"We're almost done," Justine responded.

"So, what are you two wearing to the opening?"

"Nadia is going as Edie Sedgewick, and I'm going as Andy," said Justine. "We already got the perfect wigs."

"Good idea, I like it."

"Why don't you go as Nico. You could pull it off," Nadia proposed.

"I actually considered it, but I thought I should just wear a nice dress. I found a really hot Vivienne Westwood number on sale at Bloomies."

"Oh, good call. We love Vivienne W," said Justine while expertly wrapping the packages.

"Nice job. I'll take these to Brandon's office. He's delivering them later. Back in a few." Nina walked swiftly to the offices hoping to avoid Helen when she accidentally bumped into Jack Kowski.

"Hey, Nina, slow down. What's new, pussycat?"

"Hi, Jack, just delivering some stuff to Brandon. How about you?"

"I've been working my ass off for this Warhol gig and that bulldog Helen keeps badgering me. I don't know what her problem is. That woman has a serious personality disorder."

"I know what you mean. She's tormenting me too."

"Yeah, well, she's on my back like a rabid monkey. I need a cigarette break. Care to join me?"

"No, I can't right now. I don't want to run into Helen."

"Hey, you know the *Emerald Coast* issue you're in should be out soon. I'll let you know as soon as I hear anything."

"Thanks Jack, we'll catch up later." Nina liked Jack. He was a great guy with an electric personality, a former ad man with a Hunter S. Thompson vibe. He knew everyone in town and happened to be good friends with the publishers of *Emerald Coast* magazine.

She laughed to herself, thinking about the night they first met in the early nineties before either of them worked at the EBC. She was at Timothy Leary's last big birthday party in the Hollywood Hills where one of the many entertaining highlights were helium balloons set up in the backyard for all the partygoers, delighting Nina. Jack rambled over and bet her he could inhale more balloons than her. He was right. They kept falling on the grass laughing uproariously and formed an immediate and lasting friendship. Jack was the real deal.

***

Nina got to Brandon's office, stopped, and knocked.

"Who is it?"

"It's me, Nina."

"Come on in, glad you decided to *knock*. What's in the bags?" he asked.

"These packages are for Christina Horchow. She, uhh, would like you to deliver them tonight, along with the Diebenkorn."

"She couldn't take them herself?'

"No. I guess she wanted your *personal touch*."

"What's that supposed to mean?"

"Well, I don't suppose you have ever addressed her as *Mistress Christina*?"

"What? You've got to be kidding," he chuckled.

"C'mon, Brandon, you have to admit it's not hard to imagine her in a dominant get up."

"Now that you mention it, she really could pull off a black vinyl corset and black leather thigh high boots with that hot little bod of hers. Great visual," Brandon allowed.

"Who knows, maybe she's been waiting for you to bring out her kinky side and as far as Hank's concerned, you could just put a muzzle on the old geezer. He'd probably like it," Nina went on.

"Yeah, tie him up and stick him in the glass elevator," he laughed at the idea.

"Oh, by the way, don't forget our little deal," Nina reminded him with a wink.

"Don't worry, I already e-mailed some of your images to my guys. It's in the works. I should be able to get you that review too. After all this, I think you're going to owe me a little favor."

"Okay, how about I give you my 'Beauty in Bondage' piece? It's one of the smaller black and red ones."

"Yeah, I like that one. It's a deal. So, what are you wearing to the opening?"

"A little black Vivienne Westwood dress I just picked up at Bloomies."

"Very nice. So, tell me, who paid for that LBD? Your Uncle Maximillian? Heh, heh, heh"

"Very funny. On that note, I'll be off. Have *fun* tonight at the Horchow compound. Ciao."

So Many Paintings,
So Little Time

On her way to the galleries for one last lingering look at her favorite pieces, Nina strolled through the pavilion, savoring the afternoon light streaming through the high glass walls casting shadows on the enormous face of Mick Jagger. His image was in enamel on wood, an actual part of a billboard designed by Andy Warhol for the Stones' album cover "Love You Live" in '77. Somehow the previous curator had managed to acquire it, and it wound up on the biggest back wall of the EBC, making an excellent backdrop for Nina's desk. Walking past the café, she overheard a small group of college students discussing experimental and interactive videos and how art today has become an indispensible part of our world. As they sipped their cappuccinos, the dialogue continued with some veracity and eventually turned into art for art's sake. There was so much *artspeak*, discourse, and rant flowing through these museum walls. She longed to be alone and drink in the art on her own terms.

She stopped briefly in front of the colorful timeline, which chronicled art from the turn of the century to the present. It was a real crowd pleaser, especially with the students. It made their museum experience more interesting since the galleries were not chronological but were arranged thematically. She moved swiftly past the California impressionism exhibit to the minimalism and here, surrounded by the light and space of Robert Irwin and Don Flavin, a sense of calm and weightlessness came over her. Basking in the cool temperature of the gallery, she gazed at an immense canvas created with all-white gradations of shimmering micro-glass, a huge jewel of minimal glamour by Mary Corse. She loved this painting and hoped to someday own one of hers. Too bad Maximillian would never buy it for her. His taste was so much more traditional. He preferred figurative and naturalism, with the exception of a Warhol silkscreen print of Marilyn Monroe that she'd had her eye on.

Next stop, Craig Kauffman. She thought his newer works were really exquisite. They were very sexy shapes like large oval dishes with candy in the center made of acrylic plastic, all lacquered and glittery in warm shades of pink and gold. She found them to be quite mood elevating and wondered if Craig was still living in the Philippines with his wife and kids. She moved on to the Mark Rothkos, staring at the big, overlapping bands of scarlet, orange, and yellow; she could definitely get lost in these horizons of glorious color. She made herself keep going, though, and found herself in front of a wild and wonderful Jackson Pollock.

This could require more viewing time in order to fully enjoy the countless layers of emotional splatter. *So many paintings, so little time.*

Off to Ed Ruscha's silkscreen prints with lots of floating text. Fixating on one with the Hollywood sign, Nina realized that, for her, looking at particular works of art was a lot like hearing a song that triggered a memory or a time in one's life, a visual that could be so ingrained as to have the same effect. She enjoyed studying the metamorphosis of an artist's work throughout his or her life and knew that she hadn't come close to reaching the high point of her own artistic creativity.

She made one last stop at Sylvie Fleury's chrome-plated Vanity case and Gucci Mules on white furry pedestals, so sexy and stylistic, blurring the boundaries between art and fashion. Her kind of girl, she thought. Suddenly, drenched in inspiration, she was ready to dash home and whip up some new work when Angie came rushing toward her.

"I've been looking all over for you; Spa Luxe is on line two. It's very important, something about overbooking tomorrow's appointments."

"Oh, *mon dieu*, I better get that straightened out right away."

***

Nina got on the phone ready for beauty battle. "Yes, I booked the Mediterranean deep tissue full body massage, the pacific sea salt scrub, the vanilla crème body polish, the paradise seaweed masque, and the anti-aging oxygen facial. What do you mean there's no time for hair and nails? I don't think you understand, I *have* to get my nails done, and I am desperate for highlights. Okay, okay, how about a partial? Can't you squeeze that in? All right, I'll skip the cut and the seaweed masque. Thank you. Hey, what about my whirlpool time with all the essential oils? Yeah, fine, bye. Whoa, close call."

"Oh, Nina, you are such a beauty bum," Angie laughed.

"Not really. I only go a few times a year. I've got a Spa Luxe gift card Barry gave me for Christmas that he just loaded up the other day. I'm trying to have every possible treatment I can pack in tomorrow in hopes of reaching complete spa nirvana. Well, at least emerging a new and improved version of myself. Hey, it's not easy accomplishing that much in one day!"

"I am sure you will have a fabulous day off away from Helen, relaxing at Spa Luxe."

"I intend to, but I'm going to have to get up bright and early since I plan to hit the gym first and get a good workout with my personal trainer."

"Personal trainer?" Angie asked. "I didn't know you had one."

"I can't really afford one on a regular basis. It's more like when I see her at the gym and she's available. I'm just not that disciplined, but I'll kick it up a notch when bikini season gets closer."

"Shut up and check out the guy in the parking lot getting out of the black Mercedes convertible," said Angie in a hushed tone. "He's coming this way, and he looks like your kind of man."

He blew in the door like a cool midnight breeze, about six

feet tall with tousled, shaggy hair the color of burnt sienna mixed with silver streaks. He was slim, in a white Dolce and Gabbana shirttail half untucked under a charcoal Armani jacket, with a black Prada belt, black jeans, and metallic Gucci loafers. His energy charged up the atmosphere, and Nina felt a sudden jolt of excitement. As he got closer, she guessed him to be in about his mid-fifties with a lived-in face that looked like it had plenty of stories to tell. He was sporting a Tag Heuer Monaco 69 watch and skull-shaped black titanium rings, and he definitely got their attention. Nina suspected that he was not a local. Exuding a cavalier attitude and smiling like a Cheshire cat, he moved in closer.

"Hello, ladies, looks like I came to the right place."

"Welcome to the world-famous Emerald Beach Contemporary Museum of Art," said Nina playfully. "Also known as the EBC."

"Sweet child of mine, I like the way you say that. Allow me to introduce myself. Helmut Reinhardt at your service."

"Pleased to meet you. I'm Nina Valliere, front desk concierge extraordinaire."

"I see, and a stunning one at that. Are you French?"

"Not exactly. I'm originally from Luxembourg. *Je parle francais, ein bischen Deutsch and Nederlands.*"

"Very impressive. A worldly woman at last. It must be my lucky day."

"So, Helmut, are you German?" Nina quizzed.

"German and Swiss actually. I was born in Zurich and grew up in Berlin. Seems to me we may have a lot in common. So, my beautiful Euro girl, can I get a personal tour of the Warhol exhibit from you?" asked Helmut, smelling faintly of Bulgari Aqua cologne.

"I would love to show you around. Unfortunately, the galleries are closed to the public until Sunday. I can give you an invitation for the opening reception for this Saturday if you would like to come as my guest," offered Nina.

"*C'est dommage*. I'll be in Vegas for the weekend. Is your café still open? Let's have some coffee and you can tell me your life story."

"Ha, ha, ha, we don't have time for that," Nina laughed. "It's a *very long* story, and unfortunately, I have to close up pretty soon. Tell me, what brings you to our lovely little beach town?"

"I was checking out some property in Lhana Beach, and I heard there was a big Warhol show here and thought I'd stop by on my way back to LA. So, tell me, Nina, what else do you do besides look good at the front desk?"

"I'm an artist. As a matter of fact, I'll be showing my work in a new gallery in Venice soon, and I would love for you to come to the opening. What about you, Helmut? What do you do?"

"I was in the music business for a long time, and I've been dabbling in real estate, but my passion is sculpting. I make floor sculptures out of anodized aluminum, steel, and Plexiglas. You'll have to take a look at my Web site. You know, something about you is very familiar. I have a feeling I've seen you before. Have you ever lived in LA?"

"Yes, on and off for years. I lived in Los Feliz, West Hollywood, and Hancock Park."

"Did you ever hang out at the Rainbow or On the Rox?"

Helmut asked, studying her face. "I know I've seen you before. Weren't you in, uhh, *Commando Girls?*"

"Oh my God, I can't believe you saw that movie. It was *so* bad."

"I think I saw most of the Gommarah films in the eighties that those Israeli brothers made before they went bankrupt," Helmut added.

"There was a billboard on Sunset of me and two other blonde amazons in camouflage bikinis and thigh-high stiletto boots clutching machetes promoting *Commando Girls*. It was hilarious, and went to straight to video, along with a few others I was in."

"It's all coming back to me now," said Helmut. "*Bondage Blondes* was my personal favorite. I remember you were on *Hot Rocks* on the Playboy channel in that *Kitten with a Whip* video, and there was another one. Let me think. Oh yeah, *Love Dungeon* early nineties. Well, well, well, miss *Naughty Nina*, how in the hell did you wind up here?"

"Long story, Helmut, to be continued, okay? No one here knows about any of that, and I really do have to close up the shop now."

"All right, got it, babe, but I'd like to see you again. Call me and keep me posted on the Venice show. Great meeting you," he said as their eyes locked and he pressed his business card into her hand.

"I enjoyed meeting you too, Helmut. Have fun in Vegas." She handed him a membership form with her number on it. "Let's talk next week." Watching him walk back to his car, Nina was reminiscing her LA-woman days when Angie snapped her fingers. "Hey, earth to Nina. What was all that about? Do you like that guy? He sure couldn't take his eyes off you."

"Yes, I think I do like him," she said transfixed. "I definitely need to find out more about him. Nice car too. I felt a mutual connection. I'm sure I'll be seeing him again."

***

Nina couldn't stop thinking about Helmut on the way home as she made her usual stop at the Euro-Gourmet Drive-Thru, ordering some shrimp scampi to go. She couldn't help but notice she was the only customer. Something felt eerie about the place. She would have to resort to frozen dinners from Trader Joes in the future. Once home, she went straight to the computer to look at Helmut's Web site. He had a very impressive body of work—rows of polished, cylindrical-shaped floor sculptures, circular metallic forms, sparkling wavy aluminum wall pieces. They were very dramatic and quite beautiful. Suddenly the phone machine startled her, followed by Tommy's unmistakable deep, manly voice.

"Baby doll, pick up the phone, I know you're there. It's your sweet lovin' man. C'mon, pick up. I want to see you tonight."

"Hi, Tommy. I just got home, and I'm working on a painting that a client commissioned. I've got to get up early and hit the gym and I'm following my workout with a full day of treatments at Spa Luxe. Let's skip tonight, okay, baby?"

"Oh, tough life you have," he laughed. "All right, but I miss you. So, what about the opening Saturday night. What do you want me to wear?"

"Why don't you wear the grey velvet jacket we got at Armani Exchange with your new white shirt with the French cuffs and some black jeans? Get there around seven-thirty."

The beauty of having a younger boyfriend, thought Nina, was that they were so much more manageable and didn't mind being told what to wear and what to do, unlike the older, more mature men she'd dated who were so set in their ways. She wondered what Helmut would be like.

"What are you wearing?" asked Tommy.

"I got a sexy new black dress. You'll like it."

"Do I get a private show at your place afterward? I haven't seen you dance in a while, and I have a little surprise for you," he said teasingly. Nina didn't really care for surprises. She found it somewhat juvenile, but it was typical of Tommy, and she was willing to go along with it.

"Okay, Tommy, what is it?"

"I can't tell you, baby, because then it wouldn't be a surprise, but I'll give you a hint. Yesterday, I went shopping at The Velvet Chamber and B.J. Jewelers!"

"Oooh Tommy," she brightened. "You hot, sexy man. We'll have our own private party. Get ready for a sweet ride!"

The Honorary Newfoundlander

Nina entered the Superfitness Gym in faded black yoga pants and an old Von Dutch tank, hair in a ponytail and with not a dab of makeup. Well, lipstick, of course. But that really didn't count. Her mother's motto was *never, ever* leave the house without lipstick. Nina didn't really care what she looked like at this particular gym, unlike her attire at the brand new, state-of-the-art gyms in Emerald Beach, where everyone was on the prowl in their designer workout gear. She was not out to impress anyone, socialize, or network. She just wanted to stay in shape. Heading toward the locker room, she noticed all the fitness promoting slogans; "Look Better Naked" was her favorite. After all, wasn't that why everyone was really there? A lot of soggy women of all shapes and sizes were coming out of the pool and the showers. Nina vowed *never* to go in there. There was way too much bacteria floating around. One time when the water system shut down in her townhouse she actually had to set foot in the funky, clammy shower stall and still shuddered at the thought of it.

Nothing, however, compared to showering at the YWCA in St. John Newfoundland. Due to the 9/11 chaos in 2001, en route from Brussels to Newark, her plane got diverted to the little island along with twenty-six other planes with a total of a little over five thousand passengers, more than the population of the entire fishing village. The Canadian government had to figure out where to put everyone ASAP. She wound up sitting on the plane on a small landing strip for over ten hours starving, reading Motley Crue's book *Dirt* and watching *Laverne and Shirley* reruns. They were finally bussed into the town's pride and joy, its brand-new ice hockey rink. That was *not* exactly a place where any glamour girl wanted to be on a cold Canadian night, especially without so much as a carry-on bag. Once there, everyone was given a toothbrush, coffee and doughnuts, and one blanket. Eventually groups were dispersed to various shelters, hers being a home for the disabled, catering mainly to *very large* men in wheelchairs. It was certainly not where she expected to wind up after departing from Brussels. Huge TV screens were installed to keep the frustrated and unhappy passengers informed and updated on the tragic and fatal disaster at New York's Twin Towers. After three days of this in the same outfit since nothing was allowed off the plane, a shuttle finally beckoned the ladies to the wondrous YWCA for showers. Canadian women indigenous to the area tended to be rather short and stout, and the sight of the long-legged, nude Nina with a towel the size of a kerchief was apparently something quite foreign to the regulars. Without proper moisturizing shampoo, conditioner, a wide toothed comb or even a hair dryer, it made doing her long, blonde locks nothing short of impossible.

Unhappily, but with no other option, she succumbed to a wild and wooly mountain girl look. On the fourth day, coming to the realization that she might never get off the God-forsaken island and out of sheer boredom, she took to drinking shots of Canadian whiskey in the afternoon, becoming a big hit with the locals, who in their intoxicated state, bestowed her the distinction of "honorary Newfoundlander." Sadly, she decided her only remaining option was to become a barmaid and marry a fisherman. Thankfully, on day five, after numerous and thorough searches, her plane finally took off for Newark. She never showered in a YWCA again.

Working the treadmill, she enjoyed observing the sea of tattoos on everyone throughout the gym, especially all the sexy tramp stamps on the girls. The colorful and often-curious body art generally kept her occupied for about five minutes. Nina was not one to work out too hard. This was about her limit, with the exception of going a full nine minutes once when Clive Owen was on *The View*. The big guy next to her, however, had been on twenty-seven minutes, and the sweat was really starting to fly. She hopped off to avoid the disgusting onslaught and went straight to the juice bar. She rarely even perspired, having a tendency to be a bit lazy compared to most gym enthusiasts. She thanked her lucky stars to have such a speedy metabolism. Downing a jolt of Nautilus Nitro Booster, she perked up and was ready to sprint upstairs and tackle the ultra cable cross machine. The torso rotation movement provided her with an excellent view for discreetly checking out all the good-looking guys lifting free weights. She had a thing for nicely toned arms, not too big, unlike the heavily pumped-up Russian brothers whose upper arms were so extended that they walked like muscle-mad baboons in tank shirts. They came in regularly with their own personal trainer, a short, totally buffed Asian minx, who looked like Susie Wong on steroids. She was a wicked badass, and she worked those giant Ruskies like lap dogs and had them panting and huffing and puffing, muttering swear words in Russian through every set. After watching the trio with fascination, she moved on to the butt blaster, hoping for some quick results.

While seriously working her glutes and hamstrings, she heard the unmistakable husky voice of Roxie, her busty brunette tranny trainer from Brooklyn. She was a former hair dresser, and she talked like a cross between Fran Dreschner in *The Nanny* and John Travolta in *Saturday Night Fever*.

"Good morning, Miss Nina. Are you ready for your power workout?" she asked in her distinctive Brooklyn accent.

"Yes, Miss Roxie. I had my nitro booster and a good warm up, and now I'm ready to get a six-pack just like you. I want to leave this gym with abs of steel," she laughed.

"Not so fast, Blondie. I paid good money for this physique. It doesn't happen overnight, you know. I didn't always look this fabulous," she said, admiring her curves in the floor-to-ceiling mirrored walls. It was true, Roxie had a rockin' body, extremely sculpted, a pretty face, and the firmest buns she'd ever seen, and if she could just keep her vocals up an octave, no one would ever guess that she wasn't born a woman. As far as she knew, Roxie was the only post-op tranny trainer in Emerald Beach.

"Okay, let's get to work on your ab crunches. You need to feel the *burn*."

"Go easy on me. One set is all I can handle," Nina grimaced. "Believe me, I'm already feeling the burn."

"C'mon, girlfriend, you can do it. Now I wanna see some *squats*."

"Oh God, not squats. How about a little resistance training for toning up my arms?"

"You are impossible. You're my laziest client," Roxie chided her.

"So I'm never going to be on the cover of *Muscle and Fitness*, I can live with that. Hey, you know we are having a big reception at the EBC tomorrow night. I'll give you an invitation if you'd like to go. It'll be fun."

"Oh art, schmart. What do I know from art? I'd rather go see a drag show at the Chaka Boom Room in Lhana Beach," she said, tossing her mane a la Cher.

"This is pop art, Roxie. It's an Andy Warhol Retrospect, and I think you'll enjoy it."

"I don't know, maybe. I'll think about it. Now get back to the bench and work those triceps while I get the training ball."

"No, *not* the training ball. I hate that ball."

"What am I gonna do with you?"

"Well, I haven't hit the Stairmaster yet. We can gossip and burn calories at the same time," Nina suggested.

***

After the excruciating workout with Roxie, Nina chugged a bottle of Fiji water and drove to the very posh Spa Luxe. She pulled into the circular drive to valet, and she was now entering a completely different world from the confines of the germ-laden, sweaty gym to the beautiful and elegantly pristine spa lobby. The fragrant floral arrangements and eucalyptus-infused displays created an immediate atmosphere of tranquility. The monochromatically dressed staffers spoke in hushed tones.

"Good afternoon, Miss Valliere. We've been expecting you. Would you like to enjoy your spa cuisine lunch before your first appointment?"

"Yes, I'll take it with me, thank you." As she walked on the plush, cream-colored carpeting, she noticed the decorative framed art in pale muted shades and looked forward to showering and donning the soft white terrycloth robe. Time to relax and get scrubbed, polished, and totally beautified.

All Tomorrow's Parties

The EBC was blazing with activity as Nina pulled into the parking lot. Slinging her black DKNY weekender bag out of the trunk, she ran into James walking in with an oversized coffee thermos in one hand and his crinkled Bugler tobacco pouch attached to his vegan belt.

"Ready for the big night, Nina?"

"Yes, I'm excited. I've got everything I need right here," she said, motioning to her bag. "Operation party time. You know, for glamour on the go."

"Yeah, and I've got everything I need right here too—enough caffeine and nicotine to get me through the day, which is going to be a long one," he joked. "There are some electricians at the loading dock waiting for me. I'll see you inside."

"Wait a minute, James, have you seen Helen?" asked Nina.

"She was here all day yesterday driving everyone crazy. Said she'll be in right before the VIP opening. She said her husband's coming too."

"Her husband? I can't wait to see what this guy looks like." The Spectacular Catering people arrived, and Nina accompanied them inside. The crew was still scrambling to put up the last of the signage amidst a flurry of florists and technicians. Movers brought in low-slung white plastic couches, giant screens, lighting equipment, cocktail bars and oxygen bars, a DJ booth, and go-go platforms. The place was really starting to look like a Warhol Factory for the new millennium. Nina slipped into the kitchen to see what she could rustle up before the party started, scanning the refrigerators to get an exact location on the Veuve Cliquot. She found some crab cakes and lobster rolls to tide her over. Hundreds of silver, pillow-shaped balloons were now floating up the forty-foot-high pavilion, while pulsating sounds of electronic music filled the atmosphere. Angie arrived with her garment bag, and the girls dashed in the ladies room to get dolled up and put on their new dresses.

"Damn, we look good!" announced Nina. "Let's go show James."

"You both look amazing, very nice dresses," James said, smiling.

"Thanks, James. Take some pictures of us before Helen gets here," Nina said as she handed him her little Olympus camera. They struck poses while James clicked away.

"Ohhh, here comes Helen," announced Angie.

She stormed in with two mousy young girls in tow. "These are my new interns," Helen announced. "They'll be working in the gift shop tonight. so you will need to familiarize them with the merchandise until I have time to train them properly," she said, directing her statement to Nina. "James, make sure the guards are in line tonight, and their shirts better be pressed. It's my understanding they were given dry-cleaning money this month. I don't know who in the hell authorized that expense, but I expect your boys to be on their best behavior and looking sharp!" she demanded.

"Yes, Helen, I'll see to it right away," said James. He had hired additional guards for the run of the show that were, of course, friends of Rikki and Jessie. Nina knew for a fact that Rikki hadn't washed his work shirt since last November, keeping it in the trunk of his car for convenience. Staff started streaming in, snapping up the hors d'oeuvres, champagne, and vodkatinis, commenting on the museum's glamorous transformation. Visionaries, donors and board members arrived, beautifully dressed for the initial V.I.P. reception. The Horchows made a grand entrance. Christina swept in dramatically, wearing a black-and–silver, one-shouldered, floor-length Dior gown, and Hank cut a dashing figure in his Armani tux. Amanda arrived looking very lean and elegant in her usual black Prada and headed straight for the podium. After Monty's sparkling introduction, she gave a brief speech thanking all the sponsors with a very special thanks to the Horchows. After a mild round of applause, the music started up again and the doors were opened to all the members and guests. Docents with their husbands started filtering in, followed by new members, hipster types, attractive young professionals, and the general Emerald Beach art-going crowd.

"All right, girls, I expect you to sell every one of these catalogs on display. I've got another shipment coming in tomorrow morning," Helen declared. "And be sure to put a membership application in every book." Turning to Nina, she said in a low voice, "Just between you and me, remember that Randy guy I showed you? Well, he was unfuckingbelievable. The man is amazing. I'll give you the details later, but right now I see my husband coming in." A pale, thin, sandy- haired man slid in through the throngs of guests toward the front desk.

"This is my husband, Albert."

"Oh my God, Albert, how are you?" asked Nina, surprised to see him.

"Nina, it's so good to see you again."

"Wait a minute, you two know each other?" asked Helen angrily.

"Gosh, how long has it been Albert, maybe, ten, twelve years? We had some mutual friends in LA," Nina explained.

"That's right. I think it was about twelve years ago at a party in Hancock Park. God, you look great. You haven't changed."

"Thank you, Albert. It's such a nice surprise to see you here." Helen was becoming increasingly more irritated.

"All right, you two, that's enough. Albert, go get me a cocktail and some appetizers. *Now.*"

"Okay, be right back." Poor Albert, thought Nina. He looked stressed out, just a shell of a man from what she remembered. Obviously life with Helen had taken its toll on him.

"I can't believe you know Albert. Did you ever *sleep* with him?" Helen wanted to know.

"No, Helen, of course not, we were just friends. It was before you two even met."

"Nina, here comes Tommy," said Angie. "He looks *so* cute."

Helen squealed, "That's *your* boyfriend, Tommy? My God, he's a gorgeous hunk. Where did you find him? Can I borrow him?"

"Did you already forget about Albert?" asked Nina dryly.

"Honey, you can have him. I'll take Tommy anytime. That useless husband of mine hasn't slept with me in months. I've got a little surprise for him tonight. I got my hands on some Viagra, and I'm slipping it in his drink before we leave here. If I'm not satisfied with his performance, I'll be throwing his sorry ass out on the pavement and filing for d-i-v-o-r-c-e in the morning."

"Well, that's a little harsh; Albert is such a sweet guy. I mean, you know, when I knew him before," Nina ventured.

"Stay out of it, *Pussy Galore,* and mind your own business."

"Hi, baby, you look so beautiful. I like your new dress. Hi, Angie, you sure look pretty tonight," said Tommy, charming everyone.

"You look so handsome in that jacket, Tommy," Nina gushed. "Will you please get me and Angie some champagne? Make sure it's the good stuff, baby, thanks," she said sweetly.

"You didn't even introduce me," Helen remarked. "And what's up with all the baby-baby talk with you and your dreamboat? You two sound like a Pamela and Tommy Lee sex tape. So, give it up, is he hung like Tommy Lee? Well, is he?"

"I'm not going to answer that, Helen, just stay away from Tommy."

"What's the matter? Lost your sense of humor? Ha, ha, ha," Helen howled. "I'm hungry," she said, her mood changing. "I'm going to go check up on that deadbeat husband of mine and get some grub."

Tommy eased his way back through the crowd, trying not to spill the girls' champagne.

"Who was that woman? She kept winking at me."

"That's Helen, my new boss I told you about."

"Oh no, you weren't exaggerating. It's worse than I thought. Sorry baby. Cheers girls, drink up." They clinked glasses and checked out the crowd.

All eyes went to the trendy group making a splashy entrance with a curvaceous little burgundy-haired hottie at the head of the pack, none other than Kylie Schifler, Emerald Beach's very own outspoken and totally irreverent art critic. She was known for scathing and outlandish reviews and articles, for which you either loved her or hated her. She always traveled with a complete entourage, had her own stylist, and could be seen at the chicest in crowd cocktail parties to the lowest dive bars of Toro Beach. Kylie could drink anyone under the table and still maintain her wicked sense of wit and humor. She had been covering the EBC's exhibits for years in the local *EB Weekly* and had her own EB Nitelife gossip column that covered all the dirt that had everyone practically running to a pick up a copy when it hit the stands Saturday afternoons. She had given Nina some very interesting and favorable reviews over the years, getting her some good publicity.

"Hello, Kylie, welcome to Warholwood. You are looking very scrumptious this evening."

"Thank you, Nina. You look uber lovely as always. I heard you'll be showing at the new *Hard Edge* gallery in Venice, good for you. I'll be covering it for *EB Weekly* and possibly the Venice gazette."

"Fantastic. Here is a Warhol catalog. It's on me, girl. Enjoy the show.

"Thanks, Nina, I've got a thirsty bunch here. Catch you later."

News traveled fast, thought Nina as she watched Kylie and her posse sashay toward the nearest bar. She'd better have a word with Brandon and find out more about the opening. She didn't have anything ready yet. Speak of the devil, in swaggered Brandon with a sizzling new girl, a pint-sized vintage pin up.

"Hey, Nina, looks like we're getting a great turnout. I want you to meet Chiarra. She works at Lola's Lounge in LA." The little vixen was pure candy-coated perfection.

"Nice to meet you," Nina said examining, every flawless inch of her. "You do the burlesque show in the martini glass. I've seen the ads."

"Yes, that's me. How sweet," Chiarra purred.

"We'll talk later," said Brandon, proudly whisking off his new conquest. Nina called Angie over. "Did you see that girl Brandon was with?"

"Yeah, she's amazing. How does he do it.?"

"Well, he is a pretty good-looking man, and he's talented." It was killing her not to be able to tell Angie about the S&M incident, but she was sworn to secrecy.

"Have you been keeping track of the numbers on the clicker, because we need a fairly accurate headcount for tonight?" asked Nina.

"Yeah, I've got five hundred forty so far. You know, those new interns are completely useless."

"Well, Justine and Nadia should be here soon. I'm going to go patrol, and see how everything's going out there. If you see Tommy, tell him to get us more champagne. Back in a bit." Nina inched her way through the crowd. The cocktail bars had long lines, and the buffet stations were packed with people jockeying for positions to fill up their plates, devouring the free food like they hadn't eaten all year. She spotted Tommy at the other end of the pavilion watching the screens, seemingly entertained.

"Hey, have you seen Rikki and Jessie?" she asked one of the new guards.

"No, not in awhile," he stated. "They told me to make sure that no one goes in the galleries with their drinks."

"Excellent, keep up the good work." That was probably the extent of his crash security training. She knew where to find those boys. They were probably hanging out in their private little alcove behind the kitchen. Moving past the waiters, Nina eyed an open bottle of Veuve Cliquot and helped herself, grabbing a few appetizers along the way. Once outside, she saw Rikki and Jessie laughing, beers in one hand, joints in the other.

"What are you guys doing back here? You're supposed to be in the galleries. The new guy is in there all by himself, and there's a ton of inebriated people inside."

"Hey man, chill. We got it under control. We're just getting high, no biggie. Here, take a hit," offered Rikki, laughing, handing her a joint.

"Are you kidding? I can't smoke that stuff on the job. Put those out!"

"Okay, relax. We just wanna finish our beers. James is out there patrolling," said Jessie, pushing his dyed black hair out of his eyes. "No worries."

Nina peeked around the corner and shrieked. "*Oh my God!* Those idiots are putting their drinks on top of the new Jeff Koon's piece! *Go, go, go!* Do your job *now.*

"Okay, okay, we're going." Chugging their beers, the pair darted out to the sculpture garden to apprehend the *art violators.* Moving back inside through the crowds, swigging champagne, Nina felt buzzed as she watched the go-go dancers gyrate above the swirling day-glow lights. The DJ had really cranked up the music, but seeing no sign of Tommy, she headed back to the front.

"Whoa, Angie, I just had a very close call out in the sculpture garden. I can't believe these people. Have you seen James?" she asked.

"No, I haven't, but Justine and Nadia are here now and they're selling catalogs like hotcakes." Nina turned to check them out.

"Oh wow, you girls look awesome. Love the Andy and Edie thing, good work."

"Thanks, Amanda loves it too. You know, we're running out of catalogs," Nadia pointed out.

"Don't worry there's another shipment coming tomorrow morning. So how is Amanda holding up?" Nina asked.

"I saw her on one of those white plastic couches with Jack trying to keep her propped up. One too many vodkatinis apparently," said Justine.

"It's so crowded. I never even saw Jack come in," said Nina. "He's a big man. He can carry her out to a taxi, if necessary. Hey, check it out. It looks like the late shift is coming in now." In strolled Roxie, wearing a pink feathery marabou jacket over a skintight silver lamé jumpsuit showing off lots of glittery cleavage and clear stripper shoes, arm and arm with what appeared to be a young, heavily made-up version of Candy Darling.

"Hi, Roxie. I am *so* glad you could make it. I love your outfit. You look amazing."

"Thank you, Nina, it's vintage. I picked it up in the Village ages ago. I'd like you to meet my little brother Joey. He's a hairdresser and did our makeup tonight. Doesn't he look faaabulous?"

"Hi, Joey, you look so beautiful, just like Candy Darling," Nina observed.

"Thank you. I can do your hair sometime if you like," he said, batting big false eyelashes.

"I would love that. Hey, I've got some people I want to introduce you to, so follow me." She took Roxie by the hand, leading the two *superstars* into the galleries, as she looked for Monty and Tyler. Finding them, Nina played her part.

"Hi, guys, I want you to meet some friends of mine, Roxie and Joey."

"You boys look very familiar," said Roxie. "Don't I know you from the Chaka Boom Room?"

"We've seen you on the dance floor," said Monty as he and Tyler laughed in unison. "And who is this lovely creature with you?" asked Monty.

"This is my little brother Joey. He just started doing the drag shows at the Chaka Boom Room. You gotta go on Thursday nights."

"Excuse me, but I've got to leave all of you and get back to the frontlines. Talk to you later, Roxie," Nina said, departing.

"Angieeee. How many now? What's the count?"

"Over seven hundred, but it's definitely tapering off now. Think Helen will let us go early?"

"I don't know. Depends on her mood and how anxious she is."

"What do you mean?" asked Angie.

"Let's just say she has big plans for tonight. Oh look, here she comes dragging poor Albert behind her."

"Well, girls, how did we do tonight?"

"We sold a ton of catalogs, Warhol shirts, and some memberships. The headcount's over seven hundred, still clicking."

"Excellent," said Helen in a good mood. "Albert and I need to get home. We are planning our own party, aren't we, Albert?" she said, nudging him in the ribs. The poor man looked ill. "Close everything up and I'll see you all bright and early in the morning. Don't do anything I wouldn't do," she cackled.

"Bye, Nina, really nice to see you again," he barely squeaked.

"Bye, Albert, take care."

"Poor bastard. He looks like he's going to his execution."

"Let's get Justine and Nadia to close up. I'm ready to find Tommy and go home."

"I'm right here, baby, right behind you. What a great show. I really had a good time. I met your friend Roxie. You never told me you had a personal trainer. She's really funny, killer bod too. I've never seen a girl built that solid," said Tommy innocently.

"Well, there's a reason for that."

"What do you mean?"

"I'll tell you later. It's been a long day, and I'm ready to kick off these Jimmy Choos and jet home."

"Sounds good to me. I'm ready for that sweet ride you promised me."

"That's right, baby, let's stop and pick up a couple of Redbulls on the way."

***

Rummaging through Nina's kitchen cupboards, Tommy found a pair of beautiful baccarat crystal champagne glasses.

"Hey, baby, I've never seen these before. Where did you get them?"

"Maximillian gave them to me a long time ago. He's uhh … a friend of my mom's. So, Mr. T., you sexy man, what are we drinking too?"

"You and me, baby. Cheers! I can't wait for you to open my

presents. Let's go upstairs. I'll get the lighting and the music on while you get changed."

"Okay, sounds like an excellent plan. Bring up the bottle in that silver ice bucket." They ran up to the bedroom, charged with excitement. The Redbull champagne combo had kicked in, and Tommy jumped into DJ party mode.

"Here's your package, baby, hope you like it," he said with a wicked smile as he handed it to her. Nina went into the dressing area, sipping her drink, and opened the Velvet Chamber bag. Inside the hot pink wrapping paper was a tiny white sequin bikini and white vinyl thigh-high stripper boots.

"Good God, this is some get up, Tommy," she called out. "You must be expecting some very sexy pole work.

"Good thing I went to the gym yesterday," she said to herself.

"There's more. Look for the box at the bottom." Digging under the paper, she found a little gold box. She opened it carefully, and a soft black pouch spilled out with a sparkling diamond bracelet.

"Oh my God, Tommy! I can't believe it, *I love it*!" she squealed.

"Those are real diamonds, baby. C'mon out, I want to see you."

"Put on 'Darling Nikki,' the Foo Fighters' version, and I'm on my way." She finished off her champagne and pranced out, hair swinging, shaking her ass and her wrist to show off her new bracelet, glittering in the black light. Grabbing the pole, she tossed her head back and did a butterfly swing, laughing and spinning, then executed an upside down corkscrew, sliding to the floor. She writhed her way up against the pole, back arched, and caressed herself teasingly. She kicked her long legs in the air, and the little white bikini sparkled like Christmas lights. She climbed up the top of the pole and did a firefly spin, landing in full splits right at the end of the song. Tommy, in a frenzy, was hooting and hollering on the edge of the bed.

"That was awesome, baby. *I love you!*"

Purring all the way, Nina did a wildcat crawl over to the bed and started to give him a lap dance, grinding like there was no tomorrow and feeling no pain. "*Whoooo hooooo party time,*" she shouted. Rolling and tumbling across the big bed, they caught their reflections in the mirror and ravaged each other. "Give it to meee, baby, *oh yeahhh.*"

***

The alarm went off like a bullhorn in Nina's ear.

"Oh shit, we have to get up."

"It's too early. I don't have to go to work today," growled Tommy sleepily.

"Well I do, and I *have* to be on time! You kept me up half the night with all that *rock star lovin'.* C'mon, Tommy, get up and make some coffee while I take a shower."

"Damn, girl, take it easy. You loved it and you know it."

"Yeah, well, I made you a happy man too. Let's move it, and *please* find me some Tylenol. My head is *killing* me."

"Hey now, I gave you a diamond bracelet, remember?"

"I know, baby, and I *love, love, love* my bracelet. You are an *amazing man*. Now please get me some me some coffee and cereal." Throwing on her makeup hurriedly after she finished her breakfast, she got dressed, kissed him, and ran out the door.

"Bye, Tommy, lock up before you go. Love you."

Requiem for a Playhouse

Hordes of people flocked to the front of the museum waiting for the doors to open. They really came out of the woodwork for this show, she thought, wondering if they didn't have anything else to do on a Sunday morning. Helen was already at the front desk, which was *not* a good sign.

"Good morning, Helen."

"Don't good morning me. You are *late* and you know it!" she said, scowling.

"But you know I was here working late last night and—"

"Cut the crap, Nina. You and Angie left right after I did. Justine and Nadia closed up. I am manning the desk today, and you, my dear, hah, can stay in the gift shop and help my new interns."

"I take it last night didn't go so well with you and Albert?"

"That's an understatement. I threw his useless pansy ass out on the driveway this morning and changed the locks. We are *done*. He is going to wish he'd never been born."

"Whoa, that's pretty harsh. I'm sorry to hear that," said Nina, feeling bad for Albert.

"You're looking a little rough around the edges this morning," Helen remarked, getting a closer look at Nina's puffy eyes. "Did your young stud keep you up all night?"

"Uhh, yeah, actually, we were up pretty late. We had a great time," said Nina with a smile, remembering the previous night's activities.

"I bet you did, and wipe that smile off your face. Wait a minute, let me see that little sparkler on your wrist. Is that a *diamond* bracelet?"

"Yes, it is. Isn't it beautiful? Tommy gave it to me last night."

"Oh, that's it. I didn't even get so much as a quick screw from Albert and that young hunk of burning love of yours gives it to you good and throws in a diamond bracelet! I have had it with you. Don't even talk to me. Go open the front doors, and *stay out of my way*," Helen barked.

Nina motioned the guards to open the doors and retreated to the gift shop. Feeling somewhat exiled, she attempted to make small talk with the new girls, but they were completely clueless. She did her best to stay upbeat and handle the rapacious crowd that simply could not get enough Warhol merchandise. The stuff was literally flying off the shelves. James strolled over as calm as always.

"What's going on? Has Helen banished you to the gift shop for the day?" he asked.

"She is a total witch today. She won't let me near the front desk. She won't even let me take a break. I can't wait 'til this day is over."

"Hang in there, because I've got some good news for you."

"Great, I could use some cheering up. Did I win the lottery?" Nina kidded.

"No. I just left Jack's office, and he had just gotten off the phone with the publisher at *Emerald Coast* magazine. The new issue will hit the stands tomorrow, and apparently everyone there is raving about your four-page spread."

"Oh my God, James, that is good news. I can't wait to see it."

"Jack said he would stop by their offices after work and pick up a couple of issues and drop them off here first thing in the morning," James noted.

"Fantastic, I feel better already. I think I'm going to have to pick up a nice bottle of scotch for Jack. How's it going out in the trenches?"

"It's crazy in the galleries, absolutely packed. I've got all the boys on the job today. I better get back and supervise. I'll check in later."

"Thanks, James, you made my day." One of the little interns timidly approached Nina. "Excuse me, umm, Helen said she wants to talk to you, something about some phone calls. She seems pretty upset." *Oh great, now what's wrong?* thought Nina as she hurried off.

"Yes, Helen, what is it?'

"Right now, on the *busiest* day of the year, your men are tying up the phone lines!"

"My men? What do you mean?"

"How about Tommy on line one and Maximillian on line two. What do you think this is, your personal dating central service?" Helen raged. "Have you forgotten about the *no* personal calls policy?"

"Sorry, Helen, I don't know why they called here. I assure you it will *never* happen again."

"You better believe it, Missy, because your days are numbered here. You got that?"

"Yes, I hear you, I got it. Please stop calling me Missy." Nina ducked into the ladies room, turned on her cell phone, and called Tommy.

"Tommy, what's up? Helen said you called."

"I'm still at your house and I didn't know if you wanted me to wait for you to get home."

"No, don't wait for me. I'm tired, my head hurts, and Helen's on the warpath."

"Sorry, baby. I'll make some chicken pasta for you before I go. I miss you."

"Thanks, Tommy, miss you too. I really can't talk now. I'll call you later." He sure was a sweet guy. She didn't think they made them like that anymore. Nina was starting to feel guilty about the bracelet. She knew he couldn't afford it and wondered how he was paying for it. And what about Maximillian? Why was he calling her at work? He was supposed to be in Vienna. She quickly dialed his number.

"Hello, Maximillian, it's Nina. How are you? Is everything okay? I thought you would be in Vienna by now."

"My darling girl, I've had a change in plans. I postponed my flight, and I won't be leaving until the day after tomorrow, so it's very important that I see you tomorrow night."

"Sure, where will you be?"

"I am staying at the Peninsula in Beverly Hills. My driver will pick you up tomorrow when you get home from work tomorrow and bring you here. I will explain everything when I see you."

"How mysterious. Okay, I can be ready by six."

"Excellent, champagne and caviar awaits you, my dear."

"*A demain cheri,*" she purred in her sweet, sexy French voice. *How curious,* she thought, feeling somewhat mystified. What was he really up to? The good news was she could finally drink Cristal and not have to worry about driving home. Wonder if he's sending a town car or a limo? Nina was slipping back behind the glass counters trying to avoid Helen's baleful glare when Angie popped up behind her.

"Hey, party girl, did you and Tommy have fun last night?"

"We sure did. But I feel more like slave girl today, the way FT's treating me. Look at the diamond bracelet Tommy gave me," she said, waving her wrist in Angie's face.

"Oh my God, it's *gorgeous.* I didn't think he could afford anything like that."

"He probably can't. Maximillian just called. I'm seeing him tomorrow night."

"I can hardly keep up. More diamonds for you I suppose?"

"No Angie, it's not like that."

"Oh, that's right, it's payback time for the new dress and the big deposit," Angie shot back.

"Hey, what's gotten into you?"

"I just don't think it's fair to Tommy. I mean, how long do you think you can keep up this juggling act? And what about that new guy? What's his name, Helmut?" Angie asked.

"Yes, it's Helmut. I know it's not really fair to Tommy. He trusts me, and we have so much fun together. I'm totally attracted to him. He's a great guy. Helmut, on the other hand, is more, mmm, mature, more interesting, and a little mysterious, which intrigues me. I guess I need to review my ongoing lineup of men and make some decisions."

"Yeah, and in the meantime, here comes Helen," Angie warned.

"Break it up you two," Helen ordered. "I've got enough help on the floor and we're running low on the Warhol merchandise. Nina, I need you to handle the inventory in the stockroom right now."

"Oh no, *not* the stockroom. Why can't Justine and Nadia do it?" she pleaded.

"Because *they* are helping me at the register with new members and preferred customers," snapped Helen. Feeling like a punished schoolgirl, Nina reluctantly retreated to the dusty stockroom.

Away from the action and saddled with an endless stack of inventory, she wondered how much more of this humiliation she could take. *Something's got to give and soon*, she told herself.

***

Finally home after a positively dreadful day at work, she devoured Tommy's tasty chicken pasta and decided it was time to start thinking about what to paint for the upcoming Venice show. She would simply have to sort out her increasing stable of men situation at a later date. Leaning in the doorway of her guestroom/den/studio, she gazed languorously at the paint-splattered walls. Illy espresso containers were filled with trashed brushes. Hardware store cans of bright red and black semi-gloss house paint had dripped over the edges and hardened into plastic. The floor was littered with stacks of ripped up magazines, half-used tubes of metallic acrylics, pint-size cans of varnish, and rolls of masking tape. Not a very promising sight for an emerging artist about to grace the pages of *Emerald Coast* magazine. She'd been meaning to convert her garage into a proper studio, but somehow that undertaking always stayed at the bottom of the list as much too daunting. Feeling drained, she pushed aside a gallon of gesso and flipped through a stack of paintings against the wall, nothing was popping out that seemed useable; she might have to start from scratch. She pulled out Barry's painting, a sort of *Rat Pack* collage in black and white and silver metallics, and constructed a floating frame for it. This gave it a more professional gallery look, something Brandon had taught her how to do in the workshop adjacent to the loading dock at work. Happy with her finished piece, she heard her bedroom phone ring and contemplated whether to let the machine pick up. She turned up the volume to a vaguely familiar voice.

"Hello, hello, greetings from your Vegas Viking. Reporting live from the top floor of the Mandalay Bay, sipping a tall Absolut vodka limon and tonic on ice, feeling like a midnight rambler, taking in a starry view of this city of night, city of lights, working up an appetite for a new blonde delight."

"Hi, Helmut, it's good to hear from you," she cut in. "I didn't know you were a poet too."

"Yes I am, and it's about time you picked up the phone. I could go on and on. I had a feeling you were home. How was the big opening last night?" he asked.

"It's was great, a huge success. You'll have to come back and check it out. How's Vegas?"

"Rockin' as always. I checked on my property in Summerlin, relaxed at Red Rock Canyon, had some amazing sushi at Nobu, and now I'm unwinding with a tall, cool one, not unlike yourself. So when are we getting together? I should be back in town tomorrow."

"Well, I would love to see you, but things are a little hectic at the museum right now."

"Okay, just let me know when you're ready for a moonlight drive up to my casa on Mullholland, I have a spectacular view of the city, and I just finished some remodeling. I would love for you to see the place, and I may, uhh, have some empty wall space if you know what I mean."

"Hmmm, sounds very inviting. I really enjoyed your Web site, Helmut, fantastic stuff."

"Thank you. We'll have to get one up and running for you too."

"That would be great. I just finished a painting when you called, and I'm in a fashion spread in the new issue of *Emerald Coast* magazine. It's coming out tomorrow, and there should be some images of my work in the feature too. I'll pick up an extra copy for you," Nina said cheerily.

"Congratulations. And when is the Venice opening?"

"I'm not sure, but I think it's soon, and I'm starting to get nervous about it. I'm not at all ready. I think I need some inspiration."

"I may be able to help you with that. I have been known to be very inspirational. I suggest we engage in some very carnal gamesmanship and thoroughly bad behavior and paint the town red or paint it black," Helmut cracked. "Whatever you like, name your poison. Trust me. I may be a hedonist, but I'm really a sensualist at heart, and I think we can inspire each other. Let's *collaborate*."

"That does sound intriguing. Let me think about it. I just need a good night's sleep. I'm sure things will look better tomorrow."

"Don't worry about a thing. Remember what Andy Warhol once said: 'Art is what you can get away with.'"

"I like that one. I will definitely bear that in mind. Thanks, Helmut, I think I'm inspired already. I'll talk to you soon."

"Ciao, babe, sweet dreams." She wasn't quite sure what to make of Helmut. He certainly was an interesting man with lots of boyfriend potential. Better keep him on the back burner for now. Feeling more confident about getting her act together, she stepped into a white satin slip, hit the lights, popped an Ambien, and blissfully slid in between her Egyptian sateen sheets. Sweet dreams indeed.

***

Renewed and invigorated in the cool spring air, Nina opened the doors of the EBC with a hint of anticipation. She eyed a stack of magazines on top of the desk, where James was thumbing through one.

"Good morning, Nina. Jack dropped these off earlier. You'll be very pleased."

"Oh my God, Sharon Stone's on the cover. She looks fantastic. 'Art and Fashion, The Big Mix! Great Seasonal Fashions!'" she read excitedly off the cover. "Oh, James, look, here I am on page sixty: 'EBC's finest; Nina Valliere, model/mixed media artist.' 'Ideally, I'd like to have my own combination art gallery, boutique, and lounge, as my work is continually evolving and I love mixing fashion and art,'" Nina read. "Oh God, did I really say that?"

There she was leaping across the page in a long, billowy aqua Chiffon Jil Sander evening dress, followed by a knee-skimming second skin Azzedine Alaia black sheath and black Sergio Rossi mules. She turned the page and could hardly contain herself. This was her favorite picture; on the last shoot of the day taken at the Emerald Beach Bay Club on a big yacht called Dream On, she posed on the deck in a shimmering white Balenciaga one-piece swimsuit and high-heeled strappy white sandals. At the last minute, the stylist threw her a captain's hat, and that was *the shot*. The last page featured four images of her art and a brief bio. She was more than pleased; she was ecstatic and couldn't wait for everyone to see it.

"These pictures are beautiful. There's nothing quite like professional hair, makeup, and lighting and fabulous designer clothes. I wish I could walk around looking like this every day," Nina mused.

"My personal favorite is the swimsuit. Very nautical," said James. "I like the hat too, nice touch. By the way, you'll also be happy to know that Helen won't be in until after lunch." Suddenly, a major floral delivery approached the front desk.

"Wow, who do you think these are for?" James asked with a knowing smile. A giant bouquet of exotic orchids was placed on the desk. Nina knew they were for her and they had to be from Barry. She snapped up the card which read, "Congratulations! Meet me for lunch today at the Ritz garden café, love Barry."

"I could smell those orchids all the way to sales and rental," said Angie, walking up to the desk. "I love the fragrance and they are so beautiful. Did Barry send them?"

"Yes, of course he sent them. He is always so thoughtful," Nina replied. "I'm meeting him for lunch. Did you see the magazine yet?"

"Yes, I did and the pictures are gorgeous. You're still very photogenic. You should send your mom a copy. So, big, blonde sister, let me get this straight. You've got, Barry for lunch, Maximillian for dinner, and now that Helmut guy is in the running too. When exactly do you squeeze in Tommy?"

"Angie, what's up with you? Why are you so worried about Tommy? I know I've been juggling my guys lately, but I've got to get some mileage out of this magazine while I can."

"Enjoy it now, because sooner or later someone's going to *tear your playhouse down*. Don't come crying to me if you lose Tommy."

"I'm not going to lose Tommy," snapped Nina. "I'm just working with what I've got at the moment. I'll get the man situation sorted out after tonight. Wait a minute, did you say, tear your playhouse down? Isn't that the title of a song? Yeah, I think it's called, 'I'm Gonna Tear Your Playhouse Down.' I haven't heard it in awhile, but I remember some of the lyrics. It's about a girl who has a perfect plan to get any guy she wants. Anyhow, she thinks she's got everything all set up and thinks she can get away with anything, but one of her guys sees through it and tears her playhouse right down. That's the story, Angie. Her little playhouse gets torn down *room by room*."

"It sounds like your story," said Angie.

"I've always liked that song. I can definitely identify with it. You think my *playgirl* days are numbered, don't you?" Nina asked.

"Yes I do. Just a premonition, that's all."

***

Groups of docents, museum members, and staff on their way to the galleries and the café for lunch stopped to admire the orchids and compliment Nina on her layout. She basked in their comments but had trouble getting Angie's words and the song's lyrics out of her head. Shrugging it off, she was happy to see Kylie walk in looking very sexy in low-cut Frankie B. jeans and a tight violet T-shirt with *kandygirl* in hot pink lettering across her chest.

"Hey, Kylie, good to see you. Back for more Warhol?"

"Yeah, it was too crowded the other night. Great party, though. I loved your *Emerald Coast* layout. Jack just showed it to me, very fabulous."

"Thank you, and I love your T-shirt. Shows off that hot little bod of yours."

"Oh, thanks, I just had these made for my new line of merchandise; I'm going to promote it in my next *EB Nitelife* column. We should go have drinks at Dino's and stir up a little double trouble," teased Kylie.

"Sounds like fun. Let's shoot for next weekend, and bring me a shirt."

"Okay, catch you later," said Kylie as she walked away, shooting a sassy glance over her shoulder.

***

As Nina entered the lively sunny atmosphere of the Ritz garden café, her mood brightened when she spotted Barry waving from a corner table.

"Hi, Barry, thank you so much for the magnificent orchids," she said cheerily, giving him a kiss on the cheek. "They smell wonderfully exotic and are a big hit at the front desk."

"Well, first let me tell you that your layout is absolutely stunning," he said, holding up the magazine. "I picked it up this morning on the way over. Very impressive. I love the one in the aqua dress, gorgeous shot. Maybe you can revive your modeling career. What about *More* magazine? Aren't, uhh, *mature* models back in now?"

"I have heard that. Maybe I'll give it a shot in the *classic* division. But now I think we should celebrate, don't you?" she asked, shooting him a radiant smile.

"Absolutely. Let's order seafood salads and admire this amazing layout," he proposed.

"Okay, and you'll be happy to know that I finished your painting. So, Barry, when is the champagne tasting at Dorso's?"

"Actually, Nina, that's what I wanted to talk you about. Please don't be upset, but I'm afraid we won't be able to go. My new assistant will be covering the event for me."

"What? Your new assistant? What do you mean?"

"I'm going to be taking some time off; you see, my daughter wants to go to college on the East Coast, so my ex-wife and I are going with her to check out campuses and help her get settled. We're going to spend some time in the Hamptons and get some family counseling, something we should have done a long time ago. I don't mean to throw you off course, but I'm really not sure when I'll be back." She was taken totally by surprise; this was not what she expected to hear from Barry. They had shared so much together. She thought she could always count on him. Had she taken him for granted? How could she not have seen something like this coming?

"I see. I, uhh, I don't know what to say, Barry. I guess I understand."

"Don't look so disappointed. I'm sorry, Nina, but you know it's all for the best, and we'll still keep in touch. C'mon, let's enjoy our lunch. How about a toast to the future?"

"A toast to the future? Oh sure, why not Barry?" Nina said, forcing a smile. "Here's to... our health and happiness and whatever the future may bring!"

"That's the spirit, Nina," proclaimed Barry. After pushing her food around on the plate, she couldn't sit still any longer.

"I think I better get back to work Barry. I really hope everything works out for you and your family. I'll have your painting sent to your office. Let's stay in touch. Send me a postcard from the Hamptons."

On her way out of the café, still stunned, she couldn't believe it. She had thought they were so close. One room down in her playhouse. She couldn't let it get to her. She would have to put up a brave front at work. The beat goes on. Walking back into the museum in a dark mood, the last person she wanted to see was Helen, who was waiting for her.

"Who sent you these flowers?" she screeched.

"Just a friend," replied Nina wearily.

"Well, you can tell your *friends* that if they want to send you flowers, *have them delivered to your house*. Put them in the kitchen and get these magazines out of my sight while you're at it. They have no business being all over the desk."

"Sure, Helen," Nina responded, feeling defeated. "Whatever you say."

"I'm leaving early today to pack up Albert's effects and put some things in storage."

"Albert's effects? You make it sound like he's deceased."

"Well, he's *dead* to me. You know what they say, 'One monkey don't stop the show.' Now that Albert's out of the way, I can have my new guys come over to my house. There is nothing stopping me now. I may just turn the place into a real *sex den*. I'll be juggling more men than you ever dreamed of, Miss Nina," she bragged.

"Helen, this isn't some sort of competition. No one's keeping score."

"Well, score this, you little whiner," she said, grabbing her big boobs, shaking them in Nina's face, laughing heartily. "I'll be in my office if you need me."

She watched Helen walk away and shook her head in utter disbelief. The woman was out of control, and there was nothing she could do about it. Thank God she would soon be on her way to see Maximillian.

***

At home, she peeled her work clothes off and put on a Soundgarden CD. A few slow spins around the pole made her feel sexy again. She had to get in the right frame of mind, forget about Barry, and get psyched up for tonight. After freshening up her makeup, she slathered on a rich shea butter body lotion and strategically spritzed on Cartier parfum. Wriggling into her sexiest Agent Provacateur lingerie, she stepped into her new black dress. She felt excited. She didn't know what Maximillian had in store for her, but she wanted to be as alluring as possible. She picked up the phone on the first ring, thinking it would be the driver, but she was startled to hear Tommy's voice.

"Hi, baby, what are you up to? Want some company?"

"Oh hi, Tommy, uhhh no, I've already made plans. I promised Angie to help her with, umm, that French class she's taking. How about tomorrow night?"

"I didn't know she was taking French. Well, you girls have fun, and say hi to Angie for me. Call me when you get home."

"Why don't I just call you tomorrow, baby? I'm running late. I better go. Bye, Tommy, love you." She hated lying to him, and Angie would be furious if she knew that she used her for a cover, but she would have to worry about it later. Right now she had to finish getting ready. The phone rang again; this time she let the machine answer it.

"Miss Valliere, this is Mr. Habsburg's driver, I am out front." Nina picked up. "Hi, I'll be right down, just give me two minutes." Grabbing a small black Fendi handbag, her new Jimmy Choo shoes, and the *Emerald Coast* magazine, she ran downstairs and out the door barefoot. Climbing into the backseat of the shiny black town car, she was delighted to find a mini-bar stocked with glass decanters of liqueurs and brandies. She poured herself a nice big shot of Courvoisier. Oh that Maximillian, he thought of everything. Maybe she should just pack in the whole rat race and marry the guy. She could be a Euro trophy wife, living large on *easy* street. Well, maybe not that easy. She suspected he had more than a few quirks and fetishes. He still exuded an element of mystery and probably had a dark side she had yet to explore. He certainly had bought her a lot of very sexy shoes over the years; he definitely had a thing for her slender ankles and high arches. Strapping on her shoes, feeling warm and buzzed from the cognac, she started singing the Rod Stewart song, "Tonight's the night, it's gonna be all right," when the driver cut in.

"Excuse me, Miss Valliere, we have arrived, and you are to go directly up to Mr. Habsburg's suite, 1101."

"Of course, thank you. I'm on my way," she said, feeling slightly giddy. Floating down the plush carpeted halls of the swanky hotel she felt erotically charged somehow and was more than ready for a scintillating evening. Tapping her acrylic nails on the door of Maximillian's suite, she called out playfully, *"C'est moi."* The door opened.

"Hello, my lovely Nina, wonderful to see you. Please, come in," he said, simply oozing old world charm and elegance. He was dressed in a beautifully tailored Italian beige silk suit and tan-colored Bottega Veneta shoes.

"Let me have a good look at you. Oh I love the dress, *tres jolie*, and the shoes, very, very sexy. Turn around for me so I can take in every angle, *bellisima*. Yes, very nice."

"Thank you, Maximillian. I must say, you are more handsome than ever. I am so happy to see you, and I have something for you," she said, handing him the magazine while flashing a huge smile.

"Fantastic. We will look at this together, but you must be hungry after the long drive. I have everything waiting for you."

"I am *famished*. All I had was a brandy snifter full of Courvoisier on the way, and oooh, look at this fabulous spread," she cooed. In the dining area of the deluxe suite, a sumptuous seafood tower on dry ice was filled with king crab legs, blue point oysters, jumbo shrimp, and lobster tails. A caviar station with all the trimmings was set up next to it, and in the middle was a silver ice bucket with a bottle of Cristal just waiting to be opened.

"This is amazing," she said, digging into the seafood, devouring a crab leg with one hand and scooping up a big spoonful of caviar with the other. "Sorry, I can't wait."

"No need to apologize. I adore a beautiful woman with a good appetite," he said while popping the cork. "Cheers!"

"Cheers to you, Max!" Tossing her head back, Nina finished off her flute and was ready for a refill. The bubbly liquid seared through her as the sounds of soft saxophone music filled the room. She perched seductively on an overstuffed loveseat while Maximillian poured her another glass. She was ready for *anything*. "It feels so good to be here with you," she said in her sultriest voice.

"Oui, *ma chere*. Now, let's look at your magazine layout. What stunning pictures. You are so photogenic. Very nice. Fantastic, you must send a copy to your *maman*."

"Thank you, I knew you'd like it," she beamed.

"So, how was the opening? Did it go well?"

"Oh yes, the show is a big hit. You'll have to come see it when you get back from Vienna."

"Nina, my darling, that is what I wanted to talk to you about this evening. As you know, I've had a change in plans." As lightheaded as she was, a sinking feeling of déjà vu swept over her. Wasn't that the same thing Barry said at lunch?

"But first, I have something special for you," he said gallantly.

That sounds a lot better, she thought, relieved as he left the room. What kind of gift could it be? Estate jewels perhaps? Delirious with visions of diamonds and dollars, her eyelids fluttering with joy; she thought emeralds would be nice also, to match her green eyes. Maximillian came walking toward her in what seemed like slow motion, carrying a large item covered with paper. Setting it down, he flipped the paper back to reveal a framed Warhol screen print of Marilyn Monroe.

"That's the Marilyn I've seen at your place. I don't understand," she said blankly.

"Yes it is. I know you have always had your eye on it. I want you to have it for your own collection. It's a signed, limited-edition artist's proof, very valuable. I thought you would be pleased."

"Of course I am. I love it, I … I'm thrilled to have it, thank you. Why are you giving it to me now?" she asked, somewhat puzzled.

"That is what I am trying to tell you, you see. I just sold my *pied-a-terre* here in Beverly Hills where I had the Marilyn. The rest of my collection and furnishings have already been shipped out. I have decided to move back to Vienna and take over the family business. I don't need to be in the States anymore. I didn't want to tell you on the phone, and of course, I wanted to see you before I go."

"*What?* You're moving back? I had no idea. I don't know what to say. Does that mean I, I, won't see you anymore?"

"I'll still see you. I promise to send you a ticket to Paris to visit your *maman* for her birthday this summer, and perhaps I will join you then."

"This is all so sudden," she pouted, her eyes cast downward, not able to look at him.

"Please, Nina, don't be so sad. You are very talented. You have a bright future ahead of you, and we can still keep in touch. Everything will be fine, you'll see. My driver will take the Marilyn down to the car for you. I'm sure you will find the perfect spot for her." Dazed and speechless, she slowly got up and kissed him goodbye on the cheek.

"Thank you, Max, for everything you've done for me," she mumbled.

"I will call you when I am all settled in Vienna. Take the caviar with you. It's your favorite," he said, handing her a Beluga Imports gift bag.

"Thank you, goodbye." Walking down the same halls now feeling completely shattered, she fought back the tears until she got out of the hotel. The driver put Marilyn in the trunk while she climbed into the backseat and started sobbing uncontrollably. The rooms of her playhouse were coming down, all right, one by one, just like Angie predicted. What bright future was he talking about? Apparently not one that included her in his life. Confused and hurt, she couldn't believe what just happened. It seemed so abrupt, not at all the fabulous evening she anticipated. Two men down in one day! Maximillian was her trump card, her ace of spades, her king of hearts. What the hell was going on? Apparently she'd played her cards all wrong. So much for the trophy wife fantasy. It was time to regroup and really take stock of her life. Drying her tears, she realized how much she missed her mother and would call her first thing in the morning.

Sympathy for the Devil

"Bonjour, maman. Comment vas tu?" Nina asked lovingly.

"Très bien, cherie, so good to hear from you. How is everything?"

"Everything is fine, *maman,* I saw Maximillian last night. He promised to send me a ticket to visit you in August."

"Oh, *ma fille,* it will be such a joy to see you again. I really miss you."

"I miss you too," she said, holding back her tears, "I … I'm featured in a fashion layout in a magazine. I'm going to send it to you, I'll Federal Express it so you get it right away."

"Oh mon Dieu, quel plaisir!"

"I have to go to work now. I love you, maman," she said sweetly.

"Au revoir, mon enfant."

Emotionally stirred, Nina hung up the phone and looked

fondly at a framed picture of her mother on the nightstand. Where did all those glorious years go? Her life had taken so many unexpected twists and turns. Brushing away a tear, she felt sad knowing that she would never have her own daughter to experience a mother-daughter relationship like they had. There was no room for regrets. She had to get more focused and think about the future.

Racing off to work, she made a quick stop at the liquor store to pick up some scotch for Jack to thank him for referring her for the Emerald Coast gig. She was dying to talk to Angie and tell her what happened with Barry and Maximillian. She ran directly to sales and rental when she arrived at the museum.

"Angie, you won't believe what happened yesterday. Barry told me over lunch that he's getting back together with his ex-wife and they're spending the summer in the Hamptons!" she announced.

"Oh, you're kidding. Wow, you weren't expecting that."

"No. I sure wasn't. He said they had to help their daughter find the right college and get some family counseling."

"You did have a nice long run with Barry. He's a great guy. I know you probably don't want to hear this, but I'm sure that was meant to be, and you know, it probably is all for the best," Angie shrugged.

"That's what he said too. Well, there's more. Last night I went to the Peninsula to visit Maximillian, and while I was swigging back champagne and consuming caviar like a mad woman in his ultra deluxe suite, he tells me that he just sold his place in LA and is moving back to Vienna to run the family business! I couldn't believe it. I was crushed. That's two in one day, Angie. I think your premonition jinxed me.

"Don't blame me. I think all this was bound to happen sooner or later. Looks like your playhouse really is coming down," said Angie, raising her eyebrows.

"Room by room, little sister. What's next?"

"Have you talked to Tommy?" asked Angie.

"He called when I was getting ready last night to go see Max and wanted to come over ... don't get mad, but I ... told him I was going over to your house to help you with a French lesson."

"What? You lied to him and used *me* as a cover?" Angie said, irritated.

"Hey, I'm sorry; it will never happen again, I swear. I'm turning over a new leaf."

"Oh right. I don't believe you, you're incorrigible," she said, rolling her eyes. "Poor Tommy."

"Why are you always so worried about him? He'll be fine. if I didn't know better, I'd say you have a little crush on him," Nina said, half teasing.

"Don't be silly. I know how crazy he is about you. He's a good guy, and I just don't want to see him get hurt."

"Tommy's a big boy, he'll be fine. Where is the big-lipped, man-hungry FT this morning?"

"You'll be happy to know the fierce duo went to a major museum conference in Long Beach and should be out all day."

"Excellent news," Nina said gleefully.

"What's in the bag?"

"A big bottle of scotch."

"I didn't know you drink that stuff."

"I don't, silly, it's for Jack. I'm going to run over there now. I'll talk to you later." Breezing down the halls to administration, Nina felt light and unencumbered, smiling at the staff and ready for a brighter day. Thankfully, her resilient nature had kicked in.

"Hi, Jack. I have something for you," she said, handing him the bag.

"What is it? A fifth of Johnny Walker Blue! Wow, thanks, Nina, maybe I should keep it right here in my office. The way things are going lately, we may both need a drink," he quipped.

"No kidding. I never know what to expect from Helen. One minute she treats me like a slave and the next minute she wants me to be her Internet dating confidante. It's bizarre."

"She's on a big power trip. Maybe she's bipolar," Jack reflected. "Who knows? She does seem to have some extreme mood swings. Unfortunately, our jobs are on the line thanks to that crazed road warrior."

"She's a piece of work all right," Nina agreed. "I'm going to the café. Stop by with any updates." Strolling leisurely to the café, she ran into Rikki and Jessie eating fish tacos out of a to-go box from their favorite taco stand in Lhana Beach

"Hey, guys, what are you doing here?' Nina asked. "I never see you at the front desk anymore."

"Yeah, we got chewed out for that," said Rikki. "FT told us to steer clear of the desk; she thinks we're her little whipping boys now. We can't take much more of her shit."

"Everyone's on edge because of her. Just hang in there; something's going to change soon. I can feel it."

"Hey, Nina, your cell phone's ringing," Justine called out. Nina ran to the front desk and answered on the last ring, sounding breathless, "Hello, hello."

"What a sexy voice. You should always answer the phone like that. It's Helmut. I'm back in town."

"Hi, Helmut," Nina said, catching her breath. "I literally ran from the café to the front desk to answer this."

"Because you knew it would be me, right?" he quipped. "Listen, the truth is I just can't wait another week to see you, and I've got some good news. My dealer sold two sculptures over the weekend to a new law firm in Century City, and I've signed a contract to rent out some of my work to the studios. That might be something for you to look into. Anyway, I'm having a little cocktail party at my place tonight, and I would love for you to come."

Nina glanced at her watch. "I don't know. This is pretty short notice, and it's a long, lonely drive to the Hollywood Hills."

Helmut was not daunted, suggesting, "How about we meet for sushi first? There's a great place on Sunset, the Red Geisha Den, and you can just follow me back to *mi casa*. I just had my screening room remodeled, and I can show you my new video before it goes on my Web site. I won't take no for an answer."

Nina took the bait. "Okay, you talked me into it. I'll come up. I'll call you on my way. Let's hope I don't get stuck in traffic."

She immediately regretted having agreed to go, but she didn't want to call back and cancel either. She had mixed feelings about his last-minute invitation but clearly needed to find out more about him. She had no intention of being added to his blonde-of-the-month roster. Luckily, her black dress was in the back seat of her car, and she could make a quick change. The LA blondes were fierce and plentiful, but it was time to get back in the game and restore her playhouse.

***

As she pulled up to the Red Geisha Den valet stand, the place was buzzing with paparazzi. When she stepped out of the car, she was nearly blinded by dozens of flashbulbs popping as Helmut spotted her and whisked them inside past the red velvet ropes.

"Does Paris Hilton eat here or what?" she asked, walking down a dark glossy red hall way lined with towering, multicolored Buddhas.

"Apparently there's a private party upstairs. Guess there's been some celebrity sightings. You know what LA's like. Welcome to the candy store," said Helmut, grinning. He introduced her to his art dealer and friends at a long Lucite neon-lit table littered with sake bottles, martinis, and endless trays of sushi. A tiny, platinum-haired DJ pumped up the ear-splitting techno dance music from a red-tinted glass booth while sexy little geisha girls roamed around serving sake bombs.

"Very cool place, Helmut," Nina yelled over the music. "Not the best spot for conversation though."

"I know, sorry about that. We won't stay here long. Drink up," he said, handing her a cup of burning hot sake. "Liquid energy to fuel the mind and soul. *Skoal!*" After polishing off a couple of large bottles of sake and several plates of sushi, Helmut disappeared into the crowd and Nina seized the opportunity to conduct a little investigation. Chatting up his dealer, an older, attractive, European-looking woman, Nina asked, "How long have you known Helmut?"

"I've known him a long time," she said with a German accent. "I met him when he was showing his work in Berlin, before he got into the music business. Now he's really, how do you say it? Come full circle, back to his roots so to speak, his first love: art and tall, leggy blondes."

"Really? Does he have a new blonde every month or what?"

"No, he's not really a *player*, if that's what you're trying to find out. Actually, you look a lot like his wife. She was a Swedish model. She died in a freak plane accident about five years ago.

"Oh my God, that's terrible. I didn't even know he'd been married. I really don't know too much about him."

"Helmut is very intellectual and creative and a bit, mmm, *eccentric*. He's a very complex man. I sense that both of you may share a common link. He talked about you earlier, but that's really all I can tell you. Here he comes now."

"Hey, girls, I just ran into some friends of mine and invited them up to the house. We're going over there now. So, Nina, just follow me up Laurel Canyon to Mulholland and keep your cell phone on."

Winding up the canyon, the undulating asphalt gave way to a sea of potholes as she gripped the steering wheel with each curve and dip. Passing Wonderland Avenue, she thought about all the rock 'n' roll excess that had had taken place in the past in this architectural jungle and wondered just what Helmut's role had been during that era. She had a lot to find out about him.

She pulled up to the steep driveway. His frosted glass garage door glowed from within, slowly opening to reveal a pristine interior: polished concrete floors lined with neon-lit cylindrical portals on one side and floor-to-ceiling mirrored doors on the other.

"What a stunning and immaculate garage, Helmut. Remind me to never let you see mine."

"Yes, my guys do an excellent job. I'll have to come down sometime and take a look at your place. C'mon in and meet my family," he said as he opened the door. They were greeted by two very lively Doberman Pinchers with shiny coats, one-chocolate colored and the other a more amber color.

"Meet Jojo and Whiskey. They've been with me since they were pups. They like blondes too," he joked. "They take after their old man. Don't worry, they're very friendly."

"Yes, I can see that," petting Jojo while Whiskey proceeded to lick and sniff her eagerly from all angles.

"They are great watch dogs. So, welcome to my bachelor pad. Wait 'til you see the killer view. Would you like a quick tour?"

"Yes, of course," she said, gazing at the very contemporary and impeccably furnished interiors in muted shades of taupe, charcoal and ebony. "Would you call this masculine minimalism?"

"Very funny. Actually, I like to think of it as more of an industrial Bauhaus, Zen-infused modernism Hollywood Hills executive hideaway."

"Okay," she laughed. "It's really gorgeous, Helmut. A little stark for my taste, but I love your aluminum floor sculptures. They're very dramatic, very, uh, Russian constructivism."

"How astute. I guess my modern Euro roots are showing,

and so are yours," he said, leading her out to the terrace. "Check out this magnificent view. *This* is why I love living here. So, LA woman, make yourself at home while I let my friends in."

Nina looked out at the inky blue sky dotted with sparkling stars covering the LA city skyline and thought she could probably get used to this lifestyle. She hoped that the house was *not* on stilts. She watched in awe as a black crow swooped by majestically, gliding effortlessly through the air, and knew she would have to come back in the daytime to really appreciate the view. While Helmut led his guests to the bar, she examined the various tubular wall hangings with kaleidoscopic-colored gels that offset the monochromatic interior, a playful contrast, she thought. Everything was such polished perfection; she wasn't sure if Helmut was extremely anal or just had a really good cleaning service.

"Nina," he called out. "Come and join us for cocktails." She strolled over to the black granite wet bar, surrounded by dusky beveled mirrors enveloped in soft red lighting. Its glass shelves were temptingly lined with imported vodkas, Pernod, obscure liqueurs, and vintage martini books.

"Would you like an absinthe cocktail? Helmut asked. "It's fresh in from the Czech Republic."

"Well, maybe a short one," she said, watching him prepare the milky green drinks with exacting precision. "Remember, I still have to make it back down the hill in one piece and get on the freeway without being in a complete twilight state. Very sexy bar, Helmut, but tell me, what's the foundation of this house?"

"Don't look so worried. Its bedrock, very solid, practically earthquake proof," he chuckled. "C'mon, let's take our drinks into the screening room and have a look at my video."

Nina sat next to his dealer, making small talk until the video started. Suddenly there was Helmut in animation turning into a larger-than-life artist, executing his aluminum and steel sculptural forms in various graffiti-walled factories throughout LA to the sounds of the Stones' "Sympathy for the Devil" remix. Showing off his completed series in the glaring sunlight on the rooftop of a downtown building, he then slid down a fire pole, landing in a full bar, where a beautiful, statuesque blonde handed him a chilled martini. His friends applauded and laughed as they made their way back to the bar, leaving Helmut and Nina alone in the room.

"Great video, Helmut, I really enjoyed it. I love your screening room," she said, shifting in the overstuffed black leather chair. "This chair is so comfortable. Is that a fireplace?" she asked, staring at a large metal bubble shaped object suspended from the ceiling.

"Yes, it's Swedish. Got to love the Scandinavian sense of design. So, can I freshen up your drink? How about an absinthe frappe nightcap?"

"Sounds tempting, but you know, I really should get going. I've got to be up early in the morning."

"Don't leave yet, let me get rid of my friends, I'll be right back."

Nina viewed his extensive literary, art, and film book collection, and she noticed they had a lot of the same books and definitely shared a similar taste in the arts. Also, the empty wall space looked perfectly inviting for her black-and-red paintings. Eyeing a MOCA catalog from the *Helter Skelter* exhibit, she leafed through it, regretting never having seen the show. Helmut sauntered in carrying a tall, emerald-green cocktail on ice."

"I see you're a well-seasoned drinker," she commented.

"Yes, it's taken years of practice. Why don't you join me and take tomorrow off?"

"I wish I could, but I'm not really in a position to do that. Unfortunately, my job is on the line right now and it's getting late, but I'll take a rain check," she said, reaching for her handbag.

"You better come back. You know what William Blake said: 'The Road of Excess leads to the Palace of Wisdom.' And you're in my palace now, babe."

"Yes, I'm familiar with that quote and I've been down that road a few times myself. Still waiting for all the wisdom, however."

"Aren't we all? At least let me give you a partial tour and show you what I like to call the vault. I know you will like it," Helmut persisted.

"What is *the vault*? You really have piqued my interest now; I guess I do have time for a quick look," she relented.

"Excellent. Let me show you what's behind these mirrored doors," he said while pressing a remote. The doors slowly parted to reveal a brightly illuminated room with framed gold records lining the walls and steep industrial shelving displaying an endless collection of *vinyl.*

"Holy shit." Her eyes widened. "This is awesome; it's like *High Fidelity* in here. What an amazing collection, look at all these great records. It's vinyl heaven!"

"I've been collecting since the sixties, and every record is in perfect condition. I have all the imports too. Did I mention that I was in the record business?"

"Yes you did, when I first met you," she said, browsing through the titles. "Roxy Music, T. Rex, the Sex Pistols, Mink DeVille, Iggy Pop. God, I could spend all night in here."

"I had a feeling you would appreciate it. You know, I started out scouting talent for Warner Brothers, so of course I spent a lot of time in the clubs and later got into producing and managing." He started stroking her hair, apparently feeling somewhat intoxicated by the combination of the absinthe and the scent of her perfume. "You know, Nina, you've got great hair."

"Thank you, Helmut." She shot him a sly, sexy mile and caressed his neck lightly while flipping through the records until she came to a sudden halt.

"The *Ian Blackmoor Experience*! Oh my God. I can't believe you have this record."

"Why, do you know those guys?" he asked, looking over her shoulder at the record cover.

"Do I know them? I was married to Ian Blackmoor!" she exclaimed, gaping at the record. "I need some of that green cocktail," she said grabbing his drink. "Mmm, Helmut, that's really very tasty."

"Hard to believe you were married to Ian Blackmoor."

"I met him in St. Tropez, and we got married three days later in London. Hard for me to believe now, too."

"Three days. Wow, that was a quick union. I actually met him in Manchester about ten years ago," Helmut recalled.

"*What?* You're kidding, you met Ian?"

"Take it easy babe. He was on a reunion tour, and that album has become sort of a British underground hard rock cult classic. Don't be surprised if they pop up on one of those VH1 whatever happened to them shows, without the original bass player, of course. But *your* Ian is quite talented—a little weathered but funny as hell."

"How did he look? Tell me," she implored.

"He was kind of lean and shaggy-haired with that hard-living, aging British rocker look. You know, a lot of swagger, but still very charismatic."

"Yeah, that's Ian all right," she sighed. "I wondered what happened to him. We were *so in love*, but it was a long time ago. God, I'd like to hear this record again. We had some great times. Life seemed a lot easier then, you know what I mean? I wish I didn't have to leave, Helmut, but I better get on the road while I can still drive. Can we continue this another time?"

"Of course, my lovely, leggy one," he said, gazing into her eyes. "I'm dying to spend more time with you and find out what you're all about. I'll walk you to your car and we can talk more tomorrow."

The Final Curtain

Driving down the Pacific Coast Highway toward the EBC the following morning feeling slightly hung-over, Nina opened the sunroof for a blast of fresh sea air, hoping it would invigorate her. She couldn't stop thinking about Helmut. Suddenly, she realized that she had completely forgotten to call Tommy. She felt somewhat ambivalent about both of them. It seemed as though things should be a lot clearer now with Barry and Maximillian out of the picture. She continued to vacillate between Tommy and Helmut all the way to the museum. Walking briskly inside, she went directly to the café and ordered a double red eye.

"Good morning, James," she said, perking up.

"Good morning, Nina. How are you on this gloomy spring morning? Ready for a busy day?"

"I'm a little tired, but I should be ready for anything after I finish this espresso."

Justine and Nadia slithered over like amphibian creatures right out of a *Fear and Loathing* sequence. "Hey, Nina, we have some news from Helen's *headquarters.* You are not going to like it," Justine crowed.

"Okay, I'm ready, sock it to me," Nina said gesturing with her hands in the air.

"Well, she came in early this morning in a totally manic mood and we just heard that … are you ready? Jack got the *ax.* He's o-u-t," Justine said, spelling out the letters.

"No, no, no, not Jack. Are you sure?"

"I'm afraid so. We have insider information."

"Is Amanda here? Did she authorize this?"

"We saw Helen drag her in this morning. She's probably sleeping it off in her office. The door's shut," Nadia reported.

"What's with you two? Are you EBC FBI or what?" The phone rang, and all heads turned toward it simultaneously. James slowly picked up the phone and gave Nina *the look.*

"That was Helen; she wants to see you in her office right away."

"Oh no," Nina sighed. "This may be it; *the final curtain.*"

As Nina made the dreaded walk to Helen's office for possibly the last time, highlights from the last ten years at the EBC flashed before her eyes. She smiled, remembering the good times and the bad times. Would it really be all over soon? The corridors seemed like an endless maze until she found herself right in front of Helen's office with its door wide open.

"It's about time you got here," she barked. "You've kept me waiting, and I have a very busy morning. Close the door and sit down." Swallowing hard, Nina sat down and studied Helen, sizing up the situation.

"What happened to Jack?" she asked.

"I didn't call you in here to talk about Jack. The bottom line is that this is the end of the road here for *you.*"

Tensing up, Nina asked, "What exactly do you mean by that?"

"C'mon, Nina, you must have seen this coming. Now look, I know you've been here ten years, but the fact is I've got some very serious budget cuts to adhere to, and your specific position is simply *no longer needed.* I'll be bringing in my own interns to replace you, and if the board approves a renovation, the museum will be closed for several months. So, *Ms. Nina Valliere*, your sweet little tenure here is *over.*" She smiled wickedly.

"You're really enjoying this, aren't you? What happened to the standard two weeks' notice?"

"Quite frankly, I didn't think you would need it. After all, I think I gave you plenty of warning. Don't look so shocked. You'll be happy to know that Amanda and I have prepared a nice severance check for you. Of course, you will be able to apply for unemployment as well. Won't that be fun?"

"Oh great, I can hardly wait to stand in the unemployment line," Nina replied.

"I don't think you actually stand in lines anymore, dear, but you do have to register in downtown Toro Beach," Helen snickered. "Oh, before I forget, at Amanda's insistence, you will also get two months of medical coverage! So, you're all set. Now you will have more time to juggle all your boyfriends. Good luck," she cackled gleefully.

Nina felt anger boiling up inside her, and she wanted to throw the jumbo Coke in Helen's face and tell her to go to hell. Nina wished she'd poisoned her when she still had the chance. Seething with anger and ready to strangle Helen, Nina stood up, took a deep breath, and tried to regain her composure.

"Screw you, Helen. I hope I *never* see your face again!"

"How dare you. Take your check and don't forget to get all your crap out of the front desk on your way out. Now *get out* of my office," she snarled.

Nina slammed the door behind her and stormed back down the administrative hallways for the last time. Fuming, she nearly knocked Jack's box of files over as he was coming out of the doorway of his *former* office.

"I'm sorry, Jack, I heard you got canned. I'm so furious. I just want to kill Helen."

"You too, huh? Calm down, she's not worth it. And what goes around comes around. She'll get the karma she deserves. Listen, this isn't the only game in town, babe. Let's stay in touch. Here's my cell phone number," he said, handing her his card. "Call me, I mean it. There are other gigs out there."

"Thanks, Jack, thanks for everything. I'll miss you."

"Hey, don't be a stranger. It's going to be all right. Call me anytime," he said reassuringly. "We'll get together with Kylie for cocktails."

"Okay, I'll call you."

As she walked back to the front desk, she could see James and

Angie waiting for her, knowing by the look on her face what had just happened.

"Well, guys, you guessed it, the party's over. Helen has brought down this house of cards. I'd like to kill the wretched woman."

"Sorry, Nina," said James, answering the phone. With his hand over the receiver, he said. "More bad news. Looks like you're next, Angie."

"Oh my God, I can't believe it," said Nina. "Who's going to run sales and rental? I'll wait for you, Angie." Turning to James, she said, "This is so sad."

"I'm afraid we are all replaceable."

"No, she won't get rid of you, James. She really can't replace *you*; she's not that stupid. I guess it's really time for me to pack up my stuff." As she gathered her things into an EBC tote bag, she angrily stuffed in a few extra Warhol mugs, T-shirts, and catalogs. "I'll go get my supplies out of the kitchen."

On her way back, she saw Angie talking to James and the girls. "Hey, Nina, it's all over. Helen said she's closing sales and rental. Let's get the fuck out of here. I've had enough of all the drama."

"So long, Justine and Nadia." Nina waved at the girls. "Looks like this is the perfect opportunity for you to move in for the kill and get those promotions you've been waiting for." Then she turned to James. "I'm really going to miss you. Stay in touch, and say goodbye to anyone who asks about me. I ... I don't want to cry. I better go," Nina said, tearing up.

"I just can't believe this is really happening. Maybe Amanda will snap out of it and everyone will be rehired, and she'll get rid of Helen. How's that scenario?" James asked.

"Nice try, James, but highly unlikely. Say bye to Monty and Tyler for me, and tell Brandon I'll call him in a few days."

Fighting back the tears, Nina gave James a big hug, and she and Angie walked slowly out the door, waving goodbye to everyone. She turned and stopped to take one last look at the place and felt an emotional meltdown brewing.

"What are you going to do now?" Angie asked.

"First I'm going to the bank to deposit this check. Then I'm going to the video store and pick up all the movies I haven't had time to watch this year. After that I think I'll go to Kooning Arts, then Trader Joe's, and stock up on supplies for the rest of the week. When I get home, I'm going to close the drapes, turn off the phones, maybe crack open a bottle of red wine, and throw on some Cure or Morrissey and probably cry my eyes out and basically hibernate for awhile. What about you?"

"Don't be so dramatic. It's not the end of the world. You could try another museum."

"No, Angie, I like *this* one. There aren't any other museums around here, and I'm not going to start commuting to LA."

"Okay, well, what about a gallery job. There's a new high-end commercial gallery at the mall."

"Please, don't even get me started. I've worked in those galleries and hated every minute of it. Now I don't even have Maximillian to help me out anymore. Since I can't live on unemployment checks, I really don't know what I'm going to do."

"I'm sorry Nina, now you've got me worried about you."

"Don't worry about me. I'm a survivor. I'll be fine. Hey, at least you can go back to school now. You can enroll in summer classes, and you'll have your teaching degree before you know it. I've got to go. I'll talk to you in a few days."

Nina quickly got in her car and drove off sobbing and felt sick to her stomach. She pulled over where no one could see her and reached for the Kleenex. She wasn't just losing her job and a steady paycheck; it was a lifestyle too. Her social life, all of her art connections were due to working at the EBC; all gone, just like that. Helen had steamrolled her way into the EBC and robbed her of everything she had worked so hard for. That miserable woman had *changed her life*. Her playhouse had tumbled all the way down.

Nina considered her job options and vowed that no matter how desperate, she would never again work in a high-end chain commercial gallery like the last one, where all the sales consultants were in a constant cranked-up state of anxiety, trained to pounce on every potential buyer. She could not handle the extreme sales pressure and the dreaded unjust *up system*. She had never witnessed adults so fearful to sit down or even take a lunch break or any break except for a caffeine run, refill, or a quick smoke to keep up an aggressive sales pitch in order to turn over their art-buying sheep to the manager, the almighty *closer*. He steered the hapless lot into a glass-enclosed viewing room to cast his buying spell, not unlike a cult leader hypnotizing his new victims. This was often followed by employee meetings to reveal ranking of sales from the consultants at the other galleries in the chain which Nina was, of course, always at the bottom. The ranking order created more fierce competition amongst everyone, causing an extremely edgy climate that was nerve shattering and ulcer inducing. She simply could not sell art in those conditions.

Drying her tears, feeling dejected and disheartened, Nina walked into the bank and deposited the check. *How long will it last?* she wondered. With a mortgage and car payments, her bills would soon be piling up. What about monthly beauty maintenance? It was all too depressing. Were her fearless and fabulous days over already? Sadly, lost in thought, she stopped to pick up videos, art supplies, and stocked up at Trader Joe's. She was ready to seek refuge at home.

***

As she put away her groceries, she spotted the Beluga Caviar Imports bag that Maximillian gave her and pulled out a two-ounce jar. It was much better than Haagen-Dazs anytime, in her opinion. She opened a nice bottle of pinot noir, found her porcelain spoon, and was ready to retreat to the bedroom. Angrily ripping her work clothes off, she quickly slipped into a pair of silk pajamas and closed the drapes. She turned off the volume on all the phones and put the wine and her trusty bottle of Ambiens on the nightstand. She popped in a video, a Charles Bukowski documentary she'd been meaning to watch, and settled into bed with her caviar, savoring every luscious, salty spoonful.

After a restless slumber, she awoke the following morning from a very bad dream. It was Helen in her green dress, washed ashore, covered in sand crabs and strangled in seaweed, her big fat lips blue and cracked. Bolting upright, Nina gasped at the graphic image still lingering in her head.

"Oh my God, I can't take it. Please, Lord, let me dream of anything or anyone but her," she pleaded, looking up to the ceiling. What undue wreckage had this barge of a woman brought upon her? Flying out of bed, she put on some Cure and ran downstairs to the kitchen. She felt better after a bowl of cereal and a hot cup of tea, and she decided to hang up the Marilyn that Maximillian had given her, which was still leaning against the wall. After all, it was a pretty fabulous gift, she thought as she stood back, admiring it. She would have it appraised later. Nina ran a luxurious bubble bath. She found her old harmonica and played a few bluesy tunes. She was a little rusty, but it felt good. She slid into the hot, frothy water and started singing, making up lyrics:

I woke up this mornin', feelin' so blue
I lost my job and my main man too
I gave up my heart, to the EBC
for the love of art,
but no guarantee
I gave up my soul, now I'm on the dole
I got the EBC bluuues
I'm drowning in booze
Baby, I got the EBC bluuues

She laughed to herself as she emerged from the tub. She had no idea unemployment could be so amusing. Donning a fresh pair of satin pajamas, she looked through a new, unread stack of books and pulled out *The Devil Wears Prada*. She read the back of the dust jacket, which said, "This season's must-have accessory" claimed the *Rocky Mountain News*. "A rich and hilarious new meaning to 'plaints about *The Boss from Hell*." "It's *Working Girl* meets Cruella de Ville," said *Newsday*. Well, she could certainly identify with that and dove into the book with gusto. She was not able to put it down, and she lost all track of time until she realized she hadn't eaten all day. As she pondered her future while waiting for the microwave to zap an organic lasagna, she came to the conclusion that her life didn't look too promising. She really missed talking to Barry, who had *always* been there for her. Of course, she could call Tommy, who was a good listener, and she wasn't sure about Helmut yet. Feeling emotionally fragile, she simply wasn't ready for any conversation with *anyone*.

Red lights were flashing furiously on every phone in the house, but she couldn't cope with the calls. As she walked past her computer, dinner tray in hand, she knew she should check her e-mails but couldn't look at them either; she hadn't even gone outside to collect the mail. Why bother? Not able to face reality just yet, she continued with her movie marathon and put *Sideways* in the DVD player. Propping up the pillows, she realized this certainly was the perfect film to accompany her pinot noir, which she finished by the end of the movie and blissfully passed out.

The following morning, feeling groggy and despondent, Nina barely had enough energy to get out of bed. She wondered how much longer she could go on like this and decided to write her mother a long letter. After a few pages, she thought that perhaps she should go to Paris right away to visit her. Why wait until August? She needed to get out, travel, shop, and meet new people. But for now, it was all she could do to make it to the kitchen and brew a much-needed cup of espresso.

Grabbing an armload of scrapbooks, she spread them out on the king-size bed and pored through all the great pictures taken at the EBC over the last ten years. She had posed with the girls, the guards, Monty and Tyler, James, and Angie. All the parties and opening receptions. Good times. She missed the place already and started crying all over again. This pathetic behavior had to stop; it was time to *snap out of it*. She dove back into *The Devil Wears Prada*, determined to finish the book.

Another day came to a close, and she never once looked at the clock, not knowing if it was day or night. She popped in *Croupie*r and watched it for the third time. After all, this was the film that had made her fall in love with Clive Owen. Finding her last Xanax, she swallowed it and waited to slip into oblivion.

Anarchy at the EBC

The noisy, incessant chirping of a flock of small birds in the eucalyptus trees outside of Nina's window woke her out of a deep sleep. Feeling dehydrated, she guzzled a liter of bottled water and dramatically drew open the drapes. The bright sun blazed in the bedroom, causing her to cover her eyes momentarily while she reached for the volume switch on the phone. Thirty-one messages. She prepared herself for the onslaught when the phone rang loudly. Preferring to screen the call, she waited to hear who it was.

"*Nina,* answer the phone, pick up. Pick up, it's Angie. It's an *emergenceee!*" she screamed.

"Good God, Angie, what is it? I just woke up."

"Why haven't you answered your phone? I've been calling you all morning. You won't believe what's happened. You've got to turn on COX 11 News right *now!*"

"Okay, okay, take it easy. What the hell is going on? Let me get to the TV." She grabbed the remote and flipped to channel 11.

"Breaking news," the tan, sexy brunette field reporter announced dramatically. "The body of a woman was found early this morning behind a dumpster near the Toro Beach Pier by a homeless man during his daily morning dumpster dive for recyclables. He caught the attention of a female jogger, who called 911. The woman's nude body has now been identified as forty-five-year-old Helen Boyle. She is a resident of Emerald Beach and an EBC executive."

"*What?* Oh my God! Angie, no, I can't believe it!" Nina shrieked, gasping for air while staring at the TV in shock.

"Toro Beach police spokesman, Lieutenant Bud Johnson," the anchor woman continued, "stated earlier that the body appeared bruised and may have been sexually assaulted. A suspect has not been identified as yet, and police are investigating the death as a homicide at this time. An autopsy will be performed, and the results will be released later. The county coroner cannot specify the victim's injuries or cause of death but did state that a preliminary investigation has revealed a head injury, but no bullets or stab wounds. If anyone has any information regarding the death of Helen Boyle, please contact the Emerald Beach Police Department or local Toro Beach authorities. I'm Janey Bardot with COX 11 News."

"Oh God, Angie, this is too much. I feel terrible. I mean, I actually had murder plots in my head for Helen. I just dreamt that she drowned the other night, and now she's really *dead!*"

"You had a dream that she drowned?" Angie asked incredulously. "That was a *bad* omen."

"I know, I can't believe it. This is too crazy."

"Yeah, it's crazy all right. It's unfuckingbelievable! And where have you been? I thought something happened to you. Why haven't you answered your phones?"

"I've been right here, moping around. I haven't left the house in days. I just didn't feel like talking. I have thirty-one messages on this phone and I haven't checked my cell phone or my e-mails yet. Should we call James?"

"Yeah, but I think you better check all your messages first. The EBPD will probably start questioning all the staff at the museum. You could be a suspect; everyone knows you couldn't stand her!"

"Me, a *suspect*? Wait a minute, I didn't do it. You don't really think I had anything to do with this. My God, Angie, I would never really kill anyone, even Helen!"

"All right, calm down, let me think. What about her husband? Didn't she just throw him out of the house?"

"Yes, she did, but Albert couldn't have possibly killed her. He is a really timid, sweet man. He is *not* capable of murder!"

"How can you be so sure? You hadn't seen the guy in twelve years. Maybe he's changed; maybe, he just *snapped*. It happens with the quiet ones. You hear about it all the time."

"No, no, no," Nina protested. "It must have been one of those horny online dating guys. Of course, that's it! One of those guys killed her!" she shouted.

"Did Albert know about her online dating? I think you need to contact the authorities right away."

"Oh my God, I haven't even had a cup of coffee or taken a shower," Nina wailed. "This is all too much for me right now. I don't know what Albert knew, and I'm not sure what I should do. Oh fuck, someone's on the other line. I'm afraid to answer it. Maybe it's James. I better take it. Keep the news on and I'll call you later."

"Nina, it's James," he said breathlessly. "I have been trying to reach you for days. Have you seen the news?"

"Yes, I know Helen is *dead!*"

"Yeah, she's dead all right. I have already been contacted by the EBPD, who are on their way now to question the entire staff. I have to tell you that everyone was aware of the friction between you and Helen."

"What is that supposed to mean?"

"You did say you wanted to kill her after she fired you."

"I didn't mean it!"

"I should warn you that I heard something about you wanting to poison her."

"*Poison her?* What? Are you kidding me? Who told you that?" Nina yelled.

"Everyone's talking about it. You did have more of a motive than anyone else."

"James, this is crazy. I can't even believe you would suggest such a thing! Wow, I've heard everything now."

"No, actually, you haven't. Are you sitting down?"

"Oh no, does it get worse? Is there more?" she asked, starting to panic.

"Yes, there's *a lot more,* so buckle up. After you and Angie left, Helen fired Mrs. Goldman, the accountant."

"Mrs. Goldman? Hasn't she been there for *twenty-three* years? She was just two years away from retiring."

"That's right. She was very upset, and let me tell you, things got pretty ugly. She stormed into Amanda's office, sobbing hysterically. Amanda just couldn't take it, so she slipped out the door and walked over to the Five Seasons for a bloody Mary. Evidently, she got too plastered to come back to work so she checked into one of the suites and the next morning housekeeping found her passed out on the terrace."

"Oh my God, this is some update," she said, shaking her head in disbelief.

"Hang in there, I'm just getting started," James went on. "The housekeeper called the front desk at the hotel to inform the manager of her condition, and he called us to come pick her up. So, Brandon went over there to get her, and when he saw the state she was in, he decided to check her into the Emerald Beach Pacific Promises Rehabilitation Center."

"Amanda's in rehab! Wow. Well, that probably is the best place for her."

"Well, yes, it is actually, but meanwhile we have no director, no accountant, no front desk person, and no more sales and rental. Now with Helen dead, we have no director of visitors and everything else she was running. All of her interns have disappeared, and I'm trying to man the front so I can answer the phones that are ringing off the hook."

"What about Justine and Nadia? Can't they help you?"

"Those two *muffians* have gotten very bossy and keep demanding promotions and pay increases and threatening to leave if I don't do something about it. Also, I overheard them talking about Helen's e-mails. Do you know anything about that?"

"Yes I do. The girls need to talk to the police and show them the e-mails, which should help them find out who killed Helen!" Nina was unable to contain her excitement.

"You'll have to clear that up later, because I have a lot more to tell you."

"Hold on, what about Rikki and Jessie?"

"Oh man, Helen made me fire them and told me to hire new guards from the Emerald Beach Security Agency, but they wouldn't send anyone out for the low hourly wage we offer."

"Oh my God, it's too much. I can't believe this is happening. What about their friends, Dee Dee and C.J. or whatever their names are?"

"Unfortunately, they didn't want to be here without Rikki and Jessie, so they just walked out, said they were going to start a new band."

"Who is holding down the fort in administration? Has there been a complete mutiny?"

"Monty and Tyler are toughing it out, acting very butch, but I don't know how much longer they'll last," said James.

"What about that little squeaky-voiced registrar's assistant?" Nina asked.

"Interesting you should ask, because no one has seen her since the Warhol opening. I heard she was upset about Brandon's date; remember that little vintage vixen he was with?"

"Yes, of course, you mean Chiarra."

"Right, well, I'm guessing you know more about that than I do. But more importantly, didn't you watch the local news or read the *EB Daily* paper yesterday?"

"No, I haven't been outside in days. What else have I missed? You're scaring me now."

"So you don't know what happened to Jack?"

"Jack? Oh no. Is he all right?"

"Let me have a few sips of coffee first. Okay, I hope you're ready. The day after Helen canned you and Jack, he came by to pick up some more files. So naturally, we decided to go out back and have a smoke in our little hideaway behind the kitchen. I finished my cigarette and as I turned the corner, Jack flicked his still-burning cigarette butt near the trash cans, which caught fire on an old cable leading to the kitchen's greasy grill. Maintenance had left all the paper towels on top of the grill, so while Jack and I strolled casually through the galleries, the entire kitchen burnt down!"

"Oh my God, James, I had no idea."

"The fire was all over the news yesterday. Even though it was an accident, Jack is under investigation for *arson!* Of course, we had to close down the café! Meanwhile, the maintenance guys, Manuel and Jorge, have gotten so lazy they recruited their wives to do the cleaning while they hang out at Big Daddy's Topless Club in Toro Beach. They come in whenever they feel like it, reeking of beer and so stoned, I'm lucky if I can get them to take the trash out."

"What a disaster, and poor Jack," Nina sighed.

"What about me? I'm exhausted. I can't handle this place on my own; it's out of control. I really need you to come back to work, Nina, and now that Helen is dead, why not?"

"But wouldn't Amanda have to rehire me? I'm not on the payroll anymore, and you don't even have an accountant. I think you should try to get Mrs. Goldman to come back."

"That's not possible. After the firing incident, she was so shaken that she had a mini-stroke that night, and now she's in Haine Hospital recovering. Her husband said she's out of critical condition and will be okay, but she's in no shape to come back to work. It's a mess, I tell you, and now with all the news coverage, I've got a near riot in my hands in the parking lot with people and curiosity seekers clamoring to get in."

"My God, James, I can't believe all this has gone down in three days. I leave the EBC and look what happens, complete chaos!" Nina laughed in jest. James was not amused.

"This is no laughing matter. I've got a 'temporarily closed' sign on the door for now, but I have to go talk to the crowds and tell them to go home before the police get here. Keep the news on, and I'll check in with you later. One last thing before I go. You didn't have *anything* to do with Helen's death, did you?"

"*No! I am innocent!*" she shouted.

"Okay, take a deep breath and calm down. I believe you. I'll talk to you later."

Nina sat down on the bed completely overwhelmed; she

felt drained and could barely move. She was trying to absorb everything that had happened, and she felt like a zombie as she walked slowly into the kitchen to make coffee. She turned on her cell phone and the kitchen TV, sat back, and braced herself for more bad news.

"As the investigation continues, more questions arise regarding the death of Helen Boyle, director of visitors, public relations, and special events at the Emerald Beach Contemporary Museum of Art. What was she doing at the Toro Beach pier, known for its heavy riff raff and homeless population? These questions and more will be answered. I'm Janey Bardot with COX 11 News."

Wow, that Janey Bardot sure is a stylish little hottie, thought Nina. News casting must pay well, and she gets to wear all those great clothes. Perhaps it wasn't too late to get into the business, but on second thought, she was probably too old to become an anchor woman. As she sipped her coffee and pondered the future, the phone rang, jolting her back to reality.

"Hello, hello, who is it?" she asked frantically.

"Nina, it's Albert. I have to talk to you."

"Oh my God, Albert. I was hoping you'd call. How are you holding up?"

"I am a complete wreck. I really *need* to talk you. Did Helen tell you she threw me out after the opening?"

"Yes, she was carrying on about it. I think everyone heard her."

"You don't know the half of it. The past few years with Helen have been an absolute nightmare. You have no idea how controlling she was. Anyway, I've been staying at the Motel 9 on Beach Road, and when I heard the news, I was shocked. I couldn't believe it. I thought I better get back in the house to get some of my things, but the locks were changed, so I had to break in. If the police come sniffing around here, I might be charged with breaking and entering. I'm so distraught, Nina. I swear to you, *I did not kill Helen,*" he bawled uncontrollably.

"Albert, calm down and listen to me. I never suspected you for a second. and I will tell the police that when they question me," she assured him.

"Helen was so jealous of you. She said she hated you and was going to get rid of you after she threw me out," he said, sobbing loudly.

"Yeah, well she got rid of me all right, and a lot of other people who are now jobless. The museum is a total shambles. You've got to get a grip and find her laptop. It's very important."

"It's not here; she always took it with her in the car when she went out at night, claiming she had to work late."

"Listen, Albert, there's something you need to know before it's all over the news," Nina cut in. "She hasn't exactly been working late. I'll explain later, but her cell phone and laptop should lead the police to the killer. Oh God, there's someone at the door. I have to go. Get out of there and call me later." Clutching her robe, she took a quick look in the mirror for the first time in days, a record for her. She realized there was nothing she could do about her appearance at this point and yelled out, "I'm *coming!*"

Opening the door with a big smile, Nina was confronted by two good-looking cops who were flashing their badges.

"Hi, how can I help you?" she asked pertly.

"Are you Nina Valliere?"

"Yes I am," she replied, puffing up her matted hair.

"I'm Detective Matt Miller, and this is Sergeant Brad Stone. We're investigating the death of Helen Boyle. All EBC employees are being questioned, and our special unit has been instructed to speak with you personally. Would you prefer to be questioned here or at the station?"

"Oh here, of course, please come in. How can I be of help? Would you like some coffee?" she asked sweetly. "I just put a fresh pot on."

"No thanks, ma'am."

"Please, call me Nina. Would you like some bottled water?"

"We're fine. Let's get started," Miller said. "We understand that you were with the EBC for ten years and that your supervisor was Helen Boyle, the victim in question"

"Uhh, yes, that's true," she said, noticing the other detective eyeing her disheveled appearance and sizing up the house.

"According to our information, she had you terminated on Wednesday. Is that correct?"

"Well, that's right," said Nina. "I was ... let go."

"That must have been very upsetting for you."

"Well ... yes, it was."

"Did you ever threaten her with any bodily harm?"

"What? Are you kidding? What are you getting at? I'm not a suspect am I? Am I?"

"Not yet," Miller replied. "But we do expect your full cooperation."

"I didn't kill Helen," Nina shot out. "I had nothing to with it. I haven't even been out of the house in three days!"

"Where exactly were you last Wednesday and Thursday night?"

"I just told you, I was right here. I left work Wednesday morning, made a few stops on the way home, and I haven't been out of the house since."

"Do you have a solid alibi? Do you have any witnesses?"

"No, I don't have any *witnesses*. You can check my mailbox. There's three days worth of mail out there, and look at all the newspapers piled up!"

"I'm afraid your uncollected mail is not sufficient evidence to be considered an actual alibi. Did you know the victim's husband, Albert Boyle?"

"Yes, and I can tell you that Albert is a very sweet man who wouldn't hurt anyone."

"Well, it seems the neighbors concur on that one," the other officer remarked.

"Look, I only knew Helen from work, but if you want to get to the bottom of this, then you guys need to go through her cell phone and her laptop in her car," Nina advised.

"You don't need to tell us how to do our job, Miss. We have not located the vehicle as yet. Do you have any other pertinent information you would like to share with us today?" asked Miller.

"Yes, actually, I do. I think you should know that she was very involved in a number of, uhh, adult online dating services."

"What exactly do you mean?"

"She was seeing a lot of guys from xhornymen.com and a site called wellhungnready.com."

"I don't believe I've heard of those sites," Miller said, looking at his partner. "Brad, have you heard of them?"

"No, sir, can't say that I have."

"Helen also told me that she reported a date rape from the xhornyman site not that long ago, so you should check your records," Nina persisted.

"We have checked her out. No record, no priors. There's no such report that we know of. She's only been pulled over for speeding."

"Interesting. Well, you really should check her computer at work, because she's all over those sites. She's shown them to me in her office."

"Are you saying she conducted this sort of activity at the EBC?"

"Yes, officer, I'm afraid so," Nina said, readjusting her robe.

"We will definitely look into it. Here's my card, and if you think of anything else, don't hesitate to call. And by the way, *don't leave town.*"

***

Nina ran to the kitchen in search of a quick energy boost, wolfing down a guarana bar and some vitamin B12. She could really use a shot in the ass of that stuff right now. Darting upstairs, she raced in and out of the shower as quickly as possible, washing her hair in record time. She pulled on a white Bebe Sport sweat suit, clutched her cell phone in one hand and the remote in the other, and settled back on the bed for more news.

"Investigating teams are talking with Helen Boyle's estranged husband outside their home in the upscale community of Emerald Terrace Hills," the reporter intoned. "Albert Boyle is not considered a suspect at this time." Turning to Albert with the microphone, he went on, "Mr. Boyle, can you shed some light on your wife's death?"

Visibly shaken, Albert looked ghostly white. "I, uhh, I really don't know anything."

"Did she have any enemies that you know of?"

"No, I, I, really don't know," he replied uncomfortably, avoiding eye contact.

"Thank you, Mr. Boyle," the reporter said, turning back to the camera. "As you can, see he appears to be traumatized and is in no shape for any further questioning. I'm Hunter Newman with COX 11 News. Back to you, Janey."

Janey Bardot, in a thigh-skimming, snug little Roberto Cavalli leopard dress and strappy Manolo Blanik stilettos, could now be seen questioning the neighbors as they approached her and the news van from both sides of the street. She picked out a bystander.

"Excuse me, ma'am, were you friendly with Helen Boyle?"

"Friendly? Are you kidding? That woman was a bully, always yelling, I felt sorry for that sweet husband of hers." She shook her head as a very vocal crowd of neighbors gathered around to get camera time.

"You won't see any of us putting up flowers or any kind of memorial for that witch. Good riddance!" a woman shouted.

"There seems to be a negative tone sweeping the neighborhood regarding the mysterious death of Helen Boyle as the investigation continues. I'm Janey Bardot. Stay tuned for more breaking news."

Nina's cell phone started ringing. Nina picked up anxiously, her eyes glued to the screen. "Hello?"

"Hey, it's Nadia. How are you doing? James told us he brought you up to date. It's so crazy here. Have they questioned you yet?"

"Yeah, a couple of detectives were here earlier. What about you and Justine? Did you give them those printed e-mails?"

"No, we got scared and shredded them."

"What? Isn't that destroying evidence?"

"They'll never know. Anyhow, we gave them her username and password, and they took her computer down to the station. But she had different codes for her laptop that we weren't able to get into, and that's where the real dirt is," Justine said slyly. "You know it has to be one of *those men.*"

"I know, it has to be. Hey, do you know if they found her Suburban yet?"

"I don't know, but we have full news coverage here at the museum. James is kind of freaking out because Nadia and I have pretty much taken over," she laughed.

"I have every TV in the house on. I'm watching COX 11 News right now. Isn't that Janey Bardot hot? I love her outfits; I tune in every morning before work just to see what she's wearing."

"Oh my God, we do too!" said Justine excitedly. "She is *totally* hot. Hey Nadia," she yelled out. "Guess what? Nina is a big Janey Bardot fan too!"

"We love Janey," chimed in Nadia. "Oh look, there she is in her leopard dress."

"As the EBPD continue their ongoing investigation, Helen Boyle's killer is still at large. If anyone has any information regarding this case, please contact your local authorities. I'm Janey Bardot, with COX 11 News."

"Hey, girls, I have another call coming in. I'll check in later."

"Hello?"

"Hey, it's Brandon. I've been trying to reach you. Have you seen the news?"

"Are you kidding? I'm glued to it. James told me what happened. How's Amanda?"

"She is a big *mess*. I had no idea her alcohol intake was so *extreme*," Brandon gasped. "She's going to be in rehab for a long time. You missed out on the fire. It was so crazy, and now the pavilion is covered in soot and I can't even get those fucking boneheads, Manuel and Jorge, to clean up. They're the ones who left all the paper towels on top of the grill! I feel for Jack, but you know, he shouldn't have tossed his cigarette butt. I keep telling those guys not to smoke back there. The real culprit, however, was, of course, Helen and her insane thirst for power that brought total chaos here, and now she's *dead*. It's unfuckingbelievable. So, what about you? How are you holding up?"

"I *was* in a real slump, but I've snapped out of it now. I just got questioned by a special EBPD unit, and I think I'm a suspect," Nina exhaled.

"Well, you didn't have anything to do with it, *did you?*"

"Brandon, *no!* Of course not. James asked me the same thing. Why does everyone suspect me? If I had done it her body would have wound up in the ocean, but behind a dumpster was a good place for it too. Got another call coming in. It's Tommy. Talk to you later."

"Hi, Tommy, have you been watching the news?"

"Hi, baby, yeah, I've been watching, I've been so worried about you. I've been calling for days. Angie told me what happened. Are you all right?"

"Besides the fact that I am unemployed and possibly *wanted for murder,* I'm just fine."

"Why don't I come over and look after you? I can leave right now and pick up some dinner and a movie on the way."

"That's the best offer I've had all day, Tommy. C'mon over, just give me a little time to get ready and check my e-mails."

Tommy's sexy, manly voice was always so comforting and soothing; there was something about him. He exuded a warm energy and vibe. She wasn't crazy about dating a bartender, but if he *owned* the bar and was a little older. Ahhh, why does life have to be so complicated?

Nina applied extra-volume black mascara, nude lipstick, and a flick of blush and tossed her hair upside down and gave it a good shake. Turning on her computer, she was relieved to be off the phone and away from the news for awhile to collect her thoughts. She felt besieged by the day's events and the repercussions of

Helen's actions. Still visualizing her wrapped in seaweed in *that green dress*. She was unable to shake the image until she heard those familiar three words: "You've got mail." She worked her way through the 102 emails, deleting the majority of them, and then spotted one from Helmut, a long, rambling message; she read it and deleted it, not wanting Tommy to see it. Then she noticed an email from Kylie.

Subj:EBC FIASCO!
Date:4/17/2004 10:15:37 AM Pacific Standard Time
From:kyliegirl66@gmail.com
To:ninaV009@aol.com

NINA, does Cox 11 News rock or what?? Well, my blond bodacious one, have you crawled out of the EBC's wreckage, porcelain nails intact? My sources tell me you are in the EBPD's Who Killed Helen Lineup. LOL ... well, now with those unemployment checks coming in, you'll have time to stay home and paint or write a *book* ... or at least spend more time partying with *moi* ... *Prepare* yourself ... my article covering the EBC comes out today!
Ciao for now ... Kylie, aka, Kandygirl XOXOXO

It was already Saturday, and Nina knew the *EB weekly* would be on the stands by now. She couldn't wait to see it. The paper mostly covered local current events, politics, art and film reviews, dining guides, lots of enhancement ads, and some very good articles, generally of a liberal nature. Kylie's review on the Warhol show and her usual weekly social column, which typically appeared on the last page, following the adult escort ads, should be in the new issue. But her e-mail seemed to imply something *juicier*, a special article perhaps, covering the recent craziness at the EBC.

She speed dialed Tommy and anxiously waited for him to pick up. "Tommy, stop whatever you're doing and find an *EB Weekly*!"

"I'm at Mama Gina's right now, picking up our dinner. I don't think they have any *Weeklies* here," he replied calmly.

"Then stop at The Velvet Chamber. They always have them out front."

"I'll find it, baby. See you soon."

As she paced around, waiting for Tommy, she sorted through her mail, watered the plants, and haphazardly set the table. Finally, hearing him come in, she rushed over and snatched the weekly right out of his hand.

"Oh no you don't," he said, grabbing it back. "What about a kiss first? I haven't seen you all week."

"You're right," she said, planting a big kiss on his full lips. "You sure smell good," Nina purred, stroking his toned muscular arms teasingly, "Can I see the *Weekly* now?"

"No, because I know how you are. Once you start reading, you'll ignore me and our dinner will get cold. Did you know that Mama Gina's is the best Italian food in the city?"

"No, actually, I didn't. I'm not an expert on Italian," she replied, frustrated.

"Here, have a glass of vino and relax. You look tense," Tommy said soothingly, pouring a bottle of cabernet into a decanter. "Angie told me what happened, and I want to hear all about it, but right now, let's enjoy our dinner. I'll give you a massage later."

Eating leisurely and sensually, Tommy seemed to be getting aroused. He went to the kitchen, returning with a small bag from the Velvet Chamber. "Look what I got for us baby," he said, slowly pulling out a pink satin blindfold.

"Tommy, umm, you know, I've had a hellish week, and honestly, I'm not really in the mood for a *9 1/2 Weeks* revisited right now."

"Oh, c'mon baby, I'm trying to make you forget about all that EBC stuff. It'll be fun," he pleaded, giving her his sexiest smile.

"I tell you what, just let me read Kylie's article, and then I promise to indulge your every fantasy."

"Okay, I can't argue with that. It's a deal. Here's your paper. Read it out loud so I don't have to read it after you."

"Let me see the cover," Nina said anxiously, snapping up the paper. "The Emerald Beach Film Festival—Jack Michaels screens thirty-four films and lives to review them! Oh look, here it is at the bottom of the page, 'Anarchy at the EBC,' an exclusive you don't want to miss by Kylie Schifler, page forty-three." She flipped furiously to the page. The story was splashed across in big bold print. "*Oh my God,*" she gasped.

Art Damaged

The Rise and Fall of the EBC

The Emerald Beach Contemporary Museum of Art, also known as the EBC, once a prestigious and thriving contemporary art museum in the heart of Emerald Beach, has fallen from grace and sadly, however temporarily, closed its doors. For those of you out there not familiar with its history, the EBC was created in the late '50s by a group of impassioned art lovers determined to raise the level of contemporary art culture in the OC, then often disparagingly referred to as "*The Orange Curtain.*" After a rather contentious merger with the Lhana Beach Museum and numerous minor renovations, the EBC managed to grow into a small but influential art museum presenting world-class exhibitions in all mediums from plein air, figurative to minimalism, to cutting edge installations and a proposed new media lounge.

The museum's programs for kids, art camp, and family days were always well received, and its art auctions, masquerade balls, and black-tie fundraisers are legendary. It's known for Friday night films and Rhythm and Blues Sundays and the ever-trendy Picasso Café, once an afternoon hotspot featuring tasty sliders, an exceptional wine list, and exotic coffees for all of you jacked-up art lovers.

As you probably know by now, it *burned down* Tuesday due to a freak fire in the kitchen, caused quite accidentally by none other than one of my favorite men about town, the one and only Jack Kowski, director of marketing, who was so rudely and unceremoniously terminated earlier in the week. It was an *accident,* to all the helmeted, pole-sliding jocks at the EB fire department. The EBC needs clean grills, a shout-out to shoddy maintenance. Jack, I think you owe me a *dirty martini.*

So, as I was saying, boys and girls, it seems that our EBC has come to a scandalous end indeed. After the death of the highly revered Paula Murano, the museum was without an executive director or any strong leadership, resulting in general unrest and a turnover in administration until the much-heralded arrival of a new team from the East Coast, including one lean and mean Amanda Keller and her geek squad, who took over the helm and assumed the new position. Her creative presence sent sparks flying, along with new mission statements from the board of trustees, meant to be launched globally. She attempted to provide cutting-edge art, and she was off to a great start with fundraising and helping curatorial bring us the controversial exhibit, "Girls Sheer Pop," my personal favorite; but guess what, folks? No one did their homework or a background check on Ms. Amanda. As it turned out, she has a *very* serious drinking problem, and with two or maybe it's three DUIs under her belt, it was only a matter of time before she would land in *rehab*. She's currently recovering from severe alcoholism at the lovely Emerald Beach Pacific Promises rehabilitation center. Please send flowers ASAP, people. I hear her liver's about to go!

Meanwhile, and most unfortunate for all of the EBC staff, Amanda exercised very poor judgment in hiring and promoting the power-hungry and (rumor has it) man-crazy sex addict, Mrs. Helen Boyle. And weall know what happened to her, unless you haven't tuned into COX 11 News this week, which is highly unlikely with that foxy Janey Bardot, anchor girl extraordinaire. You have to tune in just to check her out!

Well, folks, the notorious Helen Boyle, one-time shot caller at the EBC and Emerald Beach resident, was found DOA behind a dumpster near the pier in Toro Beach. That's right, *naked* and *dead!* Was she slumming in Toro bars, trolling for fresh meat? Let's hope our EPBD gets to the bottom of this one *pronto*. We haven't had a juicy murder case in our little beach community in a long time. We don't want another *unsolved mystery* on our hands. Just prior to this alarming incident, Boyle managed to fire much of the EBC staff, including the uber-elegant Nina Valliere, mixed media artist, who is also currently featured in this month's *Emerald Coast* magazine. I strongly suggest you to pick up a copy today if you haven't already. She will be sorely missed at the front desk—that is, if the museum ever reopens. The illustrious and always cool Brandon White, director of exhibitions and facilities, is now considering offers from major museums on both coasts as I write this column.

Also recovering in Haine Hospital is sixty-four-year-old Mrs. Gladys Goldman, who suffered a stroke brought on by her unexpected termination by Helen Boyle, after twenty-three years of devoted accounting. Let's all say a little prayer for her. It has also been brought to my attention that numerous administrative staff quit or simply walked out and all the interns are missing in action. Sales and rental is a thing of the past. See you in the classroom, Angie Kwan. We're always *hot for teacher.*

Representing the curatorial department, featuring "The Bald and the Buffed," are those fabulous Boom Boom Boys, Monty Black and Tyler Spikes, who were last seen heading toward

West Hollywood to open their own gallery. And for all of the young art damaged hipsters out there, your favorite and former EBC punk rock guards, Rikki and Jessie, have a new band, "The Vibes," and will be playing tomorrow night at the Python's Nest. Check it out. Beers half off before 10:00.

Last but not least, the dedicated and ever-stoic James Turner, chief of security specialist, along with his trusty Bugler pouch and never-ending supply of caffeine, is still manning the museum and *protecting the art* from any possible accidents, looting, or vandalism.

So, all you art sluts, surf hotties, hipsters, suits and socialites, docents and Abercrombie and Fitch wearing museum junkies, *life is a cabaret* and school's *out* at the EBC.

—Kylie Schifler, XOXOXOXO

Aka, Kandygirl

PS, Meet me at Dino's for happy hour. I'm ready and available for free drinks.

***

Laughing to herself with a sense of malicious pleasure, Nina dropped the *EB Weekly* to the floor, looked up at Tommy and exclaimed, *"Wow,* that little minx Kylie did it again! The rise and fall of the EBC. *I love it.* She really covered the waterfront this time. The whole town will be talking about *this* column. The phone lines should be burning up any minute now."

"No calls, baby. You promised we were going to have some fun," he pouted.

"I know, I know, but I *have* to talk to Angie. Let's call her, okay, just one quick call," she said, bubbling with excitement.

"Angie, have you read Kylie's article?"

"Oh my God, I just read it and was about to call you."

"Isn't it great? I am laughing my ass off. That Kylie ripped it up again!" roared Nina.

"I know, I loved it too," Angie chuckled.

"Hey, Tommy's here. He says he's *hot for teacher*."

"Tell him thanks a lot, I'll never live that down," said Angie. "So, what are you two up to?"

"Well, he brought over a delicious Italian dinner, a nice bottle of Cabernet, and some erotic items from The Velvet Chamber. Oh, and something about a massage later. Your guess is as good as mine," Nina said, winking at Tommy, noticing his embarrassment.

"Sounds like you two have a very sexy evening planned."

"To be continued. Details later, bye."

"What's the matter, Tommy? You look embarrassed."

"Do you have to tell Angie everything about us?"

"Of course, that's what girlfriends do. You should know that, you've watched enough *Sex and the City* with me. What's the matter, are you attracted to her?"

"Is that a trick question?"

"No, it's just that I sensed there might be something percolating between you two."

"Can we get something *percolating* between us in the bedroom?" Tommy said, stroking her thigh. "I still want to give you a full body massage, you know, to relieve you of all that post-EBC tension."

"When you put it that way, I'd say it's time to get busy and roll on up to the love shack. You can work that magic mojo."

"I'm ready baby, let's go," he said, grinning as he watched her walk up the stairs.

As she threw a white satin sheet on the bed, Nina asked, "So, what else is in that Velvet Chamber bag besides a blindfold? Let me have a look—pink fur handcuffs and a Jenna Jameson video oooh … and edible vanilla-flavored body cream. An interesting choice considering all you had to do was pick up an *EB Weekly*." She laughed playfully, wriggling out of her sweats. "Cuff me, Daddy."

"I knew you'd love it. Now let Mr. T. take over." He locked the cuffs in place and adjusted the blindfold. "That looks *very* sexy. Now open wide and taste this," Tommy urged.

"Hmmm, delicious. This is the best tiramisu I've ever had," she responded, licking her lips.

"I know, I had some on the way over. I couldn't resist," he said, popping in the Jenna tape and turning on Barry White. "Ready for more?"

"Oh yeah, give it to me … sweet strawberries. Oh yeah, give me that slow, sexy jam and mmm, mmm, mmm. Oh baby, I am loving the vanilla cream, very tasty. You know, Tommy, I have been a very *bad* girl."

"That's right, you naughty girl, talk dirty to me," he said, whipping out a paddle from under the bed. "I'm ready to *rock you hard, baby.* Hang on, *here we go.*"

***

Lying on the rumpled satin sheets, nibbling on strawberries dipped in port, and watching a *Sopranos* rerun, they were about to doze off when the phone rang.

"Your phone's ringing, baby. I was almost asleep."

"Yeah, me too. I'm exhausted, but I guess I should answer it. Might be important." Pulling the sheets up, she reached for the phone, "Hello," she rasped.

"Nina, it's me, Brandon, did I wake you up?"

"Oh, hey, Brandon, I was about to fall asleep. Have you seen the *Weekly?*"

"I sure have. I just stopped by to help James out. We both read it. My jaw dropped, and James is still shaking his head. Have you talked to Kylie?"

"No. I'll e-mail her later. What are you guys doing there this late?"

"I'm helping James keep an eye on the Warhol collection and moving everything out of the pavilion into storage. It's a big mess. There's still soot everywhere from the fire, and administration is a ghost town. By the way, I just talked to the owner at the Venice gallery, and you need to get your paintings over there ASAP. The opening is next week."

"*What?* I didn't know it was coming up so soon!"

"They need your bio and business cards and get your Web site up too," he counseled. "Don't forget, I want that *Beauty in Bondage* painting."

"Right, consider it yours; I better start slinging some paint around. Ciao. Holy Rauschenberg! I have paintings to make, Tommy. Wake up. I've got to get to work."

"What are you talking about? You're unemployed, remember?"

"I know, but I have a show coming up and I'm not ready. Will you help me?"

"Yeah, I'll help you *mañana.* I'm going back to sleep."

Nina slipped out of bed and darted into the studio and sent Kylie an e-mail.

Subj: Re: EBC FIASCO!

Date: 4/17/2004 11:10:29 PM Pacific Standard Time

From: ninaV009@aol.com

To:kyliegirl66@gmail.com

You rock … loved your column; drinks are on me at Dino's tomorrow night….

naughty Nina XOXO

The Pleasures of the Palette

As she turned on the morning news to get the *who killed Helen* update, Nina was all ears as anchorman Hunter Newman came out of the Toro Beach Police Department with his news crew behind him.

"We have a news update in the Helen Boyle investigation, whose death is still a mystery at this time," he announced. "A forty-two-year-old Joe Peters, pizza delivery man and longtime Toro Beach resident, has come forward, claiming to be the killer. After lengthy questioning, police discovered that he is, in fact, a well-known chubby chaser in the community with no criminal background. He has been under a physician's care after his recent release from the Toro Beach State Hospital's mental ward. Peters has been released and returned to his mother's mobile home, where his activities will continue to be monitored. Helen Boyle's vehicle, a bronze 2002 Chevy Suburban, has yet to be located.

Please contact authorities if you have any information regarding the vehicle. Former employees of the EBC are under suspicion at this time, police said. Stay tuned for the weather. I'm Hunter Newman, COX 11 News."

"Tommy, wake up, breaking news," she shouted. "I'm still a suspect, and a deranged chubby chaser delivered one too many triple cheese pizzas to Helen's door."

"What are you talking about? What happened?"

"Helen's killer is still at large. Maybe one of those well-hung sex maniacs got too rough with her. Where would they put her car? Think they torched it?"

"Don't play amateur detective. The cops will figure it out," Tommy reasoned. "So, baby doll, how about a little morning fun? I promise to keep it short and sweet," he said with a devious glint in his sexy hazel eyes.

"Ha, ha, ha," she bellowed, tossing her head back. "That's hilarious, Tommy. You know you're a marathon man. Sorry, I need all my energy to work on my paintings," she said, pulling on a pair of paint-splattered jeans and a T-shirt.

"Okay, I'll get out of your hair. I'm going to take off. I have to work tonight. Why don't you stop by the bar?"

"I will if I can get enough work done. I'm supposed to meet Kylie at Dino's, and we'll probably stop by later."

"You girls better behave. Love you, see you tonight."

***

Nina fastened her hair in a ponytail, arranged the boxed canvases in an assembly line fashion, slapped on the gesso, and waited impatiently for them to dry. She put on a Nina Simone CD that Barry gave her ages ago and sifted through stacks of provocative images to compile her *Belle de Nuit* series and came across two older paintings that were useable for the show. She still had three more to go. She blended the blood-red paint with a long, slender stick as the music transported her to another sphere. She dipped a brand-new brush into the thick liquid and spread it sensually on the newly primed canvas. Her paint-loaded brush flowed effortlessly across the field of white, caressing it in long, smooth strokes. She loved this shade of red; it looked and felt so erotic as it dripped onto her skin. She stepped back a few feet to examine the wide, fresh strokes; they looked so pure and clean glistening under the bright overhead lights. It felt good to have a paintbrush in her hand again. She took a deep breath and snapped her wrist, making her brush fling the paint onto the canvas like cracking a bull whip as it landed in amoeba-shaped formations. She was lost in thought, and the phone startled her; she picked up without taking her eyes off the canvas and laid the dripping brush down.

"Hello," she answered, distracted.

"Nina, it's Helmut. It's about time you answered. I've been trying to reach you for days. Didn't you get any of my messages?"

"Hi, Helmut. I'm sorry I haven't had a chance to call you back and bring you up to date. I've had a really crazy week."

"Are you all right? You sound a million light years away."

"Yeah, well, I was just painting; the Hard Edge Gallery's

inaugural opening is next week, so I'm a little preoccupied at the moment. Not to mention, I just lost my job, my boss died, the museum closed down, and I'm feeling a little lightheaded."

"Whoa, get back, Loretta. You lost your job *and* the museum closed down. What the hell happened? Do you want me to drive down there and help you out?"

"No, you don't have to do that. It's nice of you to offer, though. I'll be fine. I'm in the thick of it now, and I'm covered in paint. I'll call you later with details," she said, opening the windows.

"Promise me you'll call, or I will show up unannounced at your doorstep."

"Yes, of course I'll call you; I just need to get some work done. I promise I'll talk to you soon."

Feeling an increasing fondness for Helmut seeping into her psyche, Nina returned to the canvas lineup and plunged a big brush into the mirror glide, semi-gloss, jet black paint. She applied it evenly, admiring the thick, rich, velvety texture, while she considered the possibility of a long-term relationship with him. She was enjoying working with shiny reds and blacks; the combination looked so sleek and sexy. She continued to work on each canvas as she mused about Helmut, completely losing track of time.

She frantically tried to scrub the paint out of her acrylic nails before showering, but she finally gave up, vowing to wear surgical gloves next time. She artfully applied her makeup and blow dried her hair super straight, adding lots of glossy finishing spray, and climbed into her sexiest jeans, a black halter top, and high-heeled metallic strappy sandals. She grabbed a little silver vintage sweater at the last minute and quickly downed a tall Mount Gay rum and tonic, followed by a shot of ultra spearmint mouth spray for the road.

Dino's was packed with trendy young hipsters, local beach types, tanned silicone blondes, and a few older Italian-looking guys. It was kind of like Dan Tana's at the beach only without the industry set. The sounds of Sinatra's "I've Got You Under My Skin" filled the room, and she felt like snapping her fingers when she saw Kylie and her entourage flagging her down from a big waterfront booth.

"Hola, Nina. Hey, big sister, come join us. We're ready for refills," Kylie announced, slightly buzzed.

Nina ordered a round of drinks for the lively group, fearing this could be an expensive evening, since she knew how much Kylie could knock back.

"Great article, Kandygirl, brilliant. Let's toast to the rise and fall of the EBC."

"Yes, a toast to more *scandal* at the EBC!" shouted Kylie. "Cheers, bottoms up," she sang out as her gang followed suit, laughing their heads off. Suddenly, Jack appeared at the booth with a smirk, a glass of scotch on the rocks in one hand and an unlit cigarette in the other.

"Oh my God, look out, it's the EBC *fire starter!*" Kylie screeched to howls of laughter from the entire booth. Jack took the gibe in stride.

"Hey now, you sassy little wench, I'm a free man," Jack

retorted. "Let's celebrate. The dirty martini I owed you is on the way. Nina, babe, good to see you. How are you holding up? What are you drinking?"

"Hey, Jack, I'm okay, but this mojito could use a little freshening up, thanks. To be honest, I was pretty rattled after the whole blowout with Helen, but I'm getting back on track now. Brandon helped me get into a new gallery in Venice, but after that, who knows? What about you?"

"I have a few things brewing, nothing solid. The options diminish for a guy my age these days. I may just travel for awhile, go to Thailand and take up deep sea diving, get nomadic. Have the cops questioned you lately?" he asked, polishing off his scotch.

"Not since they showed up at my door yesterday. I'm not sure if I'm a suspect or not, but they did tell me not to leave town. Does that really mean don't leave the state?"

"I don't know, but I wouldn't head for Mexico if I were you. Seriously, I think we all need to stick around until this whole thing blows over," said Jack, chewing on his ice. "Look who just walked in. Hey girls, over here," Jack said, waving to Justine and Nadia dressed in full punk rock attire.

"Hi, Nina. Hi Jack. Hey, Kylie girl. What's up?" Nadia asked.

"My God," said Jack, shaking his head. "It's a fucking EBC reunion."

"We seem to migrate to the same places," said Justine. "You know, Jack, you actually did the place a favor by accidentally torching the kitchen. That grease joint needed to be *flushed.*

Remember that little rodent problem about a year ago? It was a Sunday morning. We had just gotten to work and heard a bloodcurdling scream and saw Nina racing out of the kitchen, completely hysterical. Rikki, Jessie, Manuel, and Jorge all went running in there and killed a giant rat and then they threw it in the trash can. We all saw it, and that sucker was huge!" she shouted, gesturing the exaggerated size of it.

"I had nightmares about it," recalled Nina. "I didn't go back in the kitchen for months."

"Here's to all the good times at the EBC!" Justine and Nadia piped in as everyone raised their glasses.

"Anarchy at the EBC!" shouted Nina jokingly. "So, what is on the agenda for you two?"

"We're still going to run the gift shop, and we just got part-time weekend jobs at The Velvet Chamber today," said Nadia.

"You are kidding me. It's around the corner from my house. Tommy and I go in there all the time."

"Well, come in and visit us. We'll give you a *discount*, just like old times." The two girls laughed in unison. "We're on our way to the Viper's Nest to check out Rikki and Jessie's new band. Want to come?"

"No thanks, I'm going to stop by the Barracuda Bar and visit Tommy, but say hi to the boys for me. Hey, Kylie, are you still thirsty?" Nina asked, observing her licking olives off her empty upside down martini glass, much to the delight of her inebriated group. "Tommy makes the best mojitos in town. Want to join me?"

"No, I'm going to stick with martinis tonight. My devoted

crew here wants to go to the Chaka Boom Room, but thanks for the drinks, and I'll definitely give you a mention in my next EB Nitelife column. I'm also covering the hottest bartenders from Toro Beach to Lhana Beach, and you can tell Tommy he'll be in the top three. *That man is so fine.* I think he looks like Clive Owen."

"Yes, I know, I'll tell him. I'll see you at the Hard Edge opening." She turned to Jack. "Hey, I'm going to take off. Think Kylie's okay?"

"Are you kidding? She's just getting warmed up. She'll be fine. Let's keep in touch."

***

She was not really in the mood for bar hopping solo, so Nina decided to run in, say hi to Tommy, have one quick drink, and go home. The Barracuda Bar was a mix of the rock 'n' roll, surf, and skater boy crowd, much too young and low-brow for Nina's swanky taste, but Tommy loved working there. She had encouraged him to apply at some of the more upscale hotel bars in town, but he wasn't particularly ambitious and seemed to be perfectly happy running the bar. His cocktail slinging talents were legendary with the locals, and a noisy bunch had gathered to watch him in action. She edged her way through the boisterous crowd as music blasted the Red Hot Chili Peppers and passed an enormous neon-lit shark tank aquarium and elbowed her way up to the bar.

"Hey, handsome, what does a girl have to do to get a drink

around here? Sleep with the bartender?" she yelled over the music.

"Hi, baby, let me fix you up with one of my world famous mojitos," Tommy said, clearly enjoying himself. "Where's Kylie? No double trouble tonight?"

"No, she and her musketeers went off to the Chaka Boom Room, but she said to let you know that you've been officially rated one of the top hottest bartenders in the region and it should be in next week's *EB Weekly*."

"Fantastic, I'll drink to that," he said, taking a quick swig of Jack Daniels. "Stick around. I'm going to light the bar on fire in a minute." Tommy had started a tradition of lighting the top counter on fire, usually around midnight when the patrons were pumped and ready to howl. It was a crowd-pleasing talent he'd picked up from The Burgundy Room in Hollywood. AC/DC came on full blast as the blue flames rocketed across the long bar, coming to a dramatic halt at the other end. The ear-deafening noise level rose to new heights, and Nina was ready for some fresh air.

"Tommy, I'm going home," she shouted.

"Want me to come over after work? I have a lot more fantasies in mind."

"I'll bet you do. Call me when you get off. If I'm still up, I'll answer."

Driving home, she found herself weighing the pros and cons of Tommy and Helmut. She adored Tommy, but he was a lot younger than her and might never get out of the bar scene. Helmut, on the other hand, was older, a successful artist, more established, and had lots of equity! She visualized herself with someone more mature and worldly and would have to make a decision. Also, there was the nasty bit of business about Helen. She didn't like being a suspect. *Who killed Helen?*

Love Is the Drug

Nina spent the next four days holed up, painting from morning until night, avoiding any and all distractions, taking breaks only for coffee, meals, and sleep. After she wired up the backs of the new paintings, she dragged them all outside and applied a high-gloss enamel coat for a vibrant finish, and they were *done*.

"Good morning, Brandon. It's Nina, everything's ready," she phoned.

"You caught me just in time; I'm on my way to the gallery now. I'll stop by and pick them up."

She lined up all the paintings for Brandon at the front door, including the "Beauty in Bondage," and waited for him, anxious of his opinion of her new work. He arrived in a no-nonsense mood and hauled them into his van without comment.

"Well, what do you think, will they sell?" she asked nervously.

"Who knows? Art buyers can be fickle, but they look good, kind of sexy. Some guy is bound to buy one."

"Oh, thanks a lot," she said, still feeling insecure.

"Don't worry, I've seen some of the other artists' work, and yours will fit right in. The gallery should get a lot of foot traffic, so I'll make sure yours get some street visibility."

"You are the *man*, Brandon, thanks for everything."

Feeling relieved and content, Nina collapsed onto the sofa as the sun's warm rays streamed in through the skylight. She watched the rays catch the crystal tears off her beautiful chandelier, causing a lovely reflection of pure light-colored hues to dart across the ceiling. *Life is good,* she thought, and she called Helmut.

"Hello, it's your long lost art starlet calling," she purred playfully.

"Finally, I've been waiting all week to hear from you. How is my mystery girl?"

"Absolutely wonderful. I finished my body of work for the show, and it's en route as we speak. I just hope some seasoned art buyers show up and purchase all of my paintings—well, at least one or two. I'm trying to be optimistic," she said with a husky little laugh.

"I am very excited to see your *body of work*. I certainly like everything I've seen so far. So, when should I get there?"

"The reception is from seven to nine, and I need to get there early, but you can come whenever you like."

"How about we meet for drinks and appetizers before the

show? There's a little French place called Marcel's Bistro within walking distance."

"That is a great idea. See you tomorrow. Ciao." Now all she had to do was call Tommy and the rest was out of her hands.

"Hi, Tommy, how's my sexy man today?"

"Hi, baby, I sure have missed you. So what's the 411 on your opening?"

"That's what I wanted to talk to you about. Do you mind going with Angie? I have to get there really early and meet the owner, and afterwards I might have to hang around and network. You know what I mean. I don't want you to get bored."

"I won't get bored; I want to go with you. I just finished your new business cards."

"I know, Tommy, but this is really important. Just this once, okay?"

"All right, I'll see you there," he said, disappointed.

"Thanks baby, see you tomorrow night." She felt terrible lying to Tommy, who certainly didn't deserve it, but what choice did she have? All she needed was a good night's sleep and the situation she'd created would hopefully seem a lot less tangled up in the morning.

***

Nina awoke to the gray light of a drizzly, overcast morning seeping in through the blinds. She hoped the coastal marine layer would lift by the afternoon. Otherwise she would have to come up with an alternate wardrobe choice for the reception. Turning on the news, she was informed of possible scattered showers for the evening but heard no updates on the Helen case. She grabbed the phone.

"Good morning, Angie. Did Tommy call you about tonight?"

"Yes, and I don't see why we can't all go together. Is that Helmut guy going?"

"Can you please just call him Helmut, and yes. You *know* I invited him."

"I also see what's going on here; you are trying to cover your ass so you can slip off with Helmut. Don't expect me to lie for you. I won't do it," she said, irritated.

"Settle down, everything is going to be fine. But just so you know, I *would* do it for you. See you tonight."

The day got increasingly dark, with ominous clouds morphing in the distance. She got an uneasy feeling that no one would buy her paintings and Tommy and Helmut would have a showdown in the gallery. Shrugging off her fears, she put on some Lenny Kravitz and tried to figure out what to wear. Glancing across the sea of black dresses in her closet, she picked out a sexy little ruched number by Marciano and pulled on a pair of high-heeled black leather boots. Zipping them up slowly, listening to the spring rain beating on the bedroom window, she decided that a black patent-leather trench coat and gloves would be the perfect accessories for the gloomy weather.

Driving north on the 405 on any given Friday afternoon could be a daunting experience, and with the rain splashing down on the windshield, she felt compelled to stay off the cell phone and concentrate on her visibility. She was thrilled to arrive at the gallery and find a perfect parking place. She dashed in and introduced herself to the owner, the *high priest*. He was a tall, thin, spiky-haired, thirty-something guy in a black suit with a lot of attitude—a total art snob; she realized that she would have never gotten in the show without Brandon's help.

A few other artists in the group show were milling around the sleek little white cube of a gallery, admiring their own paintings, chatting quietly with their friends. She smiled to herself when she saw her own group of work, which looked so much more striking under the bright lights on pristine white walls than in her messy studio. Pleased with the installation, she made a run for it to Marcel's Bistro. Helmut was already well ensconced at the bar as she approached him, shaking the raindrops off her hair.

"Hello, Helmut, it's wet out there. I see you're way ahead of me as usual."

Studying her from head to toe, his eyebrows raised, he said, "Love your espionage outfit, very Bond girl. Your sexy style is so endearing. Have you been to the gallery yet?"

"Yes, I popped in quickly and met the owner. Not much activity in there, but it's still early. I am more than ready for a drink after that rainy drive."

"Champagne and shrimp cocktails are on the way. I really have missed you, and I want to hear all about your week. I can't wait to see the show."

Nina peeled off her gloves and trench coat as slowly and seductively as possible, never leaving his eager gaze. She perched on the barstool, crossed her long legs, and flashed him a big smile.

"Ready for a toast, *mein herr*?" she asked, whipping her hair back.

"Yes I am, you saucy thing. Great boots, by the way. Let's have a toast to… low-brow art, high-brow art, Bond girls, and good living! You are white chocolate in stilettos, babe. Cheers!"

"To *la dolce vita*!" she said, tossing back the bubbly filled flute. She relished the jumbo shrimps and listened with amusement to Helmut's rambling LA gonzo-style tales of bygone Hollywood music business excess until it was time to go.

When she arrived at the gallery with Helmut, she tried to blend into the crowd before Tommy and Angie arrived. She excused herself to supposedly make small talk with the owner in order to avoid an awkward Helmut and Tommy collision. Keeping one eye on the front door, she spotted Brandon and the lovely Chiarra coming her way.

"Hey, Brandon, everything looks great. Hi, Chiarra, nice to see you again," she said, staring in awe at her flawless milky white skin and perfectly delicate features.

"Hi, Nina, I love your black and red paintings. They're so *dark and sexy*. Helmut tells me he's *very* interested in you."

"You know Helmut?"

"Of course, darling, he comes into my club. I've known him for years, and believe me, you are *his type*." Motioning for Nina to bend down within earshot, she whispered, "He is loaded. He owns homes in Benedict canyon and Malibu. He is … umm, a bit eccentric, but a real catch."

"Why thank you for sharing that with me," Nina said, inhaling Chiarra's heady perfume. Suddenly, she saw Tommy and

Angie walk in and noticed Helmut examining her paintings and chatting with the owner. Racing over to Tommy, she gave him a big kiss and whisked him over to the other side of the gallery.

"Any trouble finding the place?" she asked nervously.

"Hi, baby. It was easy to find. Here are the cards I made for you. This is a nice gallery. Do they have any good beer here?" asked Tommy casually.

"Thank you, these cards are perfect," Nina said, giving him another kiss. "The drinks are in the back. Go help yourself."

Angie shot Nina a dirty look. "What do you think you're doing, Agent 99? I see Helmut lurking on one side of the gallery, and you've just sent Tommy to the other side. I'd say your juggling skills need a little fine tuning."

"Look, I know what you're thinking, but I really like Helmut."

"What about Tommy? He talked about you all the way here," she snapped.

"Why are you so protective of Tommy? Can't you just help me out this once? I'd do it for you. Oh shit, here comes Helmut."

"Nina, I love your work," he said excitedly. "Very erotic stuff, babe."

"Oh, thanks, uhhh, you remember Angie from the museum?"

"Yes, hi, Angie, nice to see you again. I'm going to check out the liquor situation. I'll be right back."

Helmut eased his way through the crowd as Tommy walked

back holding a Corona. "Not much of a selection. I didn't see anything you would like. Let's go look at your paintings."

Angie nudged Nina, giving her a disapproving look. "What do you think? Do you like them?" asked Nina as she looked over her shoulder to see if Helmut was on the way.

"Wow, they look great," said Tommy. "What are all those red dots for?"

"That means they're *sold*!" Angie explained.

"*What?*" Nina cried out, snapping her head around. She gawked at all the red dots in disbelief, "Are you kidding me?"

"How did they sell so fast? We just got here," said Tommy.

The Hard Edge gallery owner who had been so indifferent earlier slinked over to Nina with a new attitude and tactfully let her know that all five paintings had just been purchased, with one pending because two customers wanted the same painting.

"Who bought them? I can't believe it," Nina said, completely stunned.

"I did," said Helmut, walking up to the group, grinning. Angie was speechless as Tommy interjected, "Who is this guy? Do you two know each other?"

"Tommy, this is Helmut Reinhardt, he's an art collector. We met at the museum last week."

"Hey, man, nice to meet you," said Tommy as they shook hands.

"Will you excuse us for a moment, please?" Nina said tensely, as she pulled Helmut aside. "Helmut, I never expected you to buy all my paintings."

"I know you didn't. Relax, I like them. As you do know, I have plenty of wall space. There's a guy outside who wants the one with the masked girl, 'Midnight Chloe.'"

"Oh, of course, the naked one. Well, let him have it; I can make you another one, *on the house.*"

"Great, it's a deal. Let me go finish up the transaction."

Reeling in amazement, Nina said out loud to herself, "Oh my God, I need a calculator!"

"Hey, baby," Tommy called out. "That's very impressive for one night's work. I think you should take me and Angie out for drinks. Let's go into Hollywood and celebrate."

"I would love to, Tommy, but I think I need to stay here and … talk to the owner. Why don't you and Angie go on ahead and I'll try to catch up with you later," Nina said, avoiding eye contact with Angie, feeling her disapproving glare.

"Okay, but don't take too long. Call us as soon as you're done."

"I will. I'll probably see you guys soon." Nina exhaled a sigh of relief just as Brandon, Chiarra, and Helmut strolled over.

"Well done, Nina," said Brandon. "You are on a roll tonight. Oh by the way, Kylie called me. She said she couldn't make it tonight but promised you lots of coverage."

"Thanks, I don't know what to say. I'm a little overwhelmed."

"I'm sure Helmut will enjoy his new *acquisitions,*" said Chiarra, winking at Nina as she gave Helmut a little squeeze.

"Thanks, doll, do you have a show tonight?"

"Yes, Brandon and I are going over to the club now. Do you want to meet us there?" she asked.

"No, but we'll take a rain check," said Helmut. "I think Nina and I may have other plans."

"You two have fun. Bye," she said, blowing kisses.

"I would love to see Chiarra's act," said Nina.

"I'll take you another time. I thought we should go celebrate in Vegas."

"Vegas? Tonight? Are you serious?"

"Sure , why not? We can be at LAX in twenty minutes and catch the next flight out. I do it all the time. I get comped at the Hard Rock and the Bellagio. I'll make a few calls on the way to the airport and get everything booked."

"Helmut, I don't know about going to Vegas right now. I wasn't expecting any of this," she said hesitantly, "I don't exactly have my overnight bag with me."

"Don't worry about it. We can pick up whatever you need in the shops tomorrow morning. Weren't you toasting to the good life earlier? So, *let's party!*"

"You're right," she said, getting excited. "Oh, wait a minute, I can't go. I'm not supposed to leave the state."

"What do you mean?" he asked, puzzled.

"I haven't had a chance to tell you about everything that happened this week. You see, I think I'm considered a possible suspect for the murder of my former boss, Helen Boyle. The Emerald Beach Police Department told me not to leave town, and I'm not sure if they meant the state."

"*Murder?* Oh, naughty Nina," he said, laughing. "You've got to be kidding. A sexy artist and a dangerous criminal. I love it, how fascinating."

"Hey, she fired me and two days later her dead body turned up in Toro beach. I had nothing to do with it."

"I really don't think it should keep you from going to Vegas. It's not like you're under surveillance."

"I know, but I'm sure the case will be wrapped up soon. Can't we go to Vegas another time? I would love to see Chiarra's show tonight."

"All right, I'll call and get us a VIP booth near the front. Just follow me over there."

Nina got behind the wheel, following Helmut's black Mercedes closely while calling Tommy. Feeling apprehensive, she tried to sound as normal as possible. "Hi, Tommy, are you and Angie having fun?"

"Not really. We're on our way to the Chateau Marmont Bar. Are you done yet?"

"No, it looks I'm going to be stuck here awhile, and then I'll probably have to go out for a drink with Helmut and the gallery owner."

"What's up with that Helmut guy? Why did he buy all your paintings? Does he have a thing for you?"

"No, baby, he's a collector, that's all. I just need to, you know, hang out for awhile."

"Okay, but make sure he knows that I'm your boyfriend. Do you want to talk to Angie?"

"No, no, just tell her I'll call her tomorrow. Have fun. Bye." Feeling incredibly guilty, her mind racing in high gear, Nina pulled up behind Helmut and slammed on the brakes at the valet stand in front of a nondescript grey building. A burly bodyguard stood under the black awning to direct them inside. As they entered the deco foyer, a blinking pink neon Lola's Lounge sign beckoned customers with a life-size poster of Chiarra. A sparkling little boutique with her line of vintage lingerie and accessories was prominently displayed.

"Oh my God, we have to shop in here. Helmut, look at all this sexy stuff, I love it," she cooed, poring through racks of one-of-a-kind retro corsets, slips, bras, and marabou jackets.

"I like these stretchy little black satin shorts," said Helmut, holding them up for Nina's approval. "They would look great with your boots. What size are you?"

"I'm usually a medium. They are so cute. I'm sure they will fit. What about this sequined corset and elbow-length gloves and … oooh, rhinestone collar?"

"You *are* giving me a private show tonight, aren't you?" Helmut asked, stroking her hair.

"Yes, as a matter of fact, I am going to give you the ultimate VIP treatment, Master Reinhardt," she said with a little laugh.

"Now you are talking directly to my soul, babe. You better get a Lola's Lounge T-shirt and sunglasses for the morning, because you are *not* going home tonight."

Swinging the Lola's Lounge bag of goodies, they walked hand in hand into the club, which was overflowing with sexy, young lingerie-clad waitresses and cigarette girls. An exotic brunette in a white satin bra and beaded panties led them to a leopard velvet VIP booth where Brandon was already seated.

"Hey, glad you could make it. The show's just about to start," he said coolly. Nina was amazed at Helmut's attentiveness to her in spite of all the luscious distractions in every direction, which were giving her extreme whiplash; she was more of a girl watcher than the guys.

The hot, jazzy music kicked in as shimmery pink drapes parted and Chiarra was lowered from the ceiling on a black velvet swing. Her diminutive frame glowed in the blue lighting as she tossed her rhinestone top hat to the audience and flipped over the seat, making a perfect landing on a black cabaret chair. The crowd applauded as she proceeded to peel off her glittery corset and gloves burlesque style, revealing perfectly luminous white skin adorned in bejeweled pasties and panties, a garter belt, and thigh-high stockings. Nina was in awe watching this divine creature as a giant martini glass slid across the stage and a tall Lucite ladder popped up from the floor. Chiarra climbed up and teasingly removed her garter belt, high heels, and stockings on each rung until she was completely nude at the top of the glass. She dipped her tiny arched foot into the clear liquid and submerged herself, balancing onto a giant plastic olive while blowing kisses to the audience as the curtains closed. The crowd was still applauding and howling as two curvaceous, red-haired dancers shimmied onto center stage.

"That was amazing," exclaimed Nina to Brandon . "Chiarra is absolutely exquisite. You're a lucky man."

"Yes, I know, but I've got stiff competition from a *very* wealthy suitor. I'm going back to her dressing room; I'll talk to you tomorrow."

"Let's get our own private Mulholland Drive cabaret show going. Are you ready, Nina?"

"Yes, Sir Helmut," she said nervously with a quick military salute. "I'm always ready."

***

Whiskey and Jojo seemed particularly excited to see Nina, leaping on her so enthusiastically that she tumbled to the floor with the two dogs until Helmut finally called them off.

"Sorry about that. As you already know, they take after their old man. They're just happy to see you. Let me get you a drink and you can change into those shorts."

Guzzling her drink, she wandered down the hallway in search of a guest room where she slipped into the corset, gloves, and shorts to the sounds of "Funky Cold Medina." As she hooked up the rhinestone collar, she stared at her reflection in the mirror and wondered what the hell she was doing. *It's too late now*, she thought and headed back down the hall. She could see Helmut busily whipping up cocktails at his wet bar and lining up camera equipment, singing along to the music. She decided to take a quick peek in the other rooms. The first one appeared to be a fully equipped office, but the next door she opened contained something altogether unexpected. Her eyes widened at the sight of dozens of blonde, erotically dressed mannequins in various positions throughout the room, some leaning sensuously, others seated and lounging provocatively on clear cubes and platforms. Their exquisite faces stared at her with dead, glassy eyes. *How bizarre,* she thought and wondered when he was planning to show her this particular *collection.*

"Nina, c'mon out," he yelled. "I'm getting impatient."

Grabbing a riding crop out of one of the mannequin's hands, she straightened up and gave him her best Cadillac walk, turning and posing for his viewing pleasure while he snapped away.

"Fantastic, you look outstanding., I think we got some great shots. I'll load them up on the computer later. Where did you get that crop?"

"I found it in your, uhhh, mannequin room."

"Oh, you already saw my mannequin collection. Well, what do you think?"

"I'm very intrigued. Is there any other special room you want to show me?"

"Yes, there is. The master bedroom, of course. Follow me," he said slyly, carrying the cocktails. The sprawling, sexy suite was a total bachelor fantasy, early James Bond style. He slipped into a black satin smoking jacket and propped himself up comfortably against the leather headboard. He lit up a joint and slowly sipped his drink. Nina downed her cocktail and did a sultry striptease at the edge of the bed to the sounds of Bryan Ferry's, "Love is the Drug," unhooking her corset one hook at a time. Enjoying Helmut's obvious state of arousal, she gave her corset a swift fling across the room, keeping a gloved hand across her breasts, and turned toward the wall so he could have a good look at her ass and long, slim thighs. Grinding slowly, and rhythmically to the music, she put the riding crop between her teeth and slid the little black shorts down, revealing a tiny black glittery g-string, and bent over all the way to the floor.

"I love the way you tease me, Mistress Nina," Helmut said and smiled broadly.

"If you don't behave, I'll give you a good caning," she said, whipping around toward him with a feline gait, smacking the crop against the palm of her hand. "You're in trouble now."

"Keep talking and keep the boots on, babe, that's the way I like it."

***

Finally falling asleep at dawn, Nina had restless dreams, tossing and turning for a few hours until she was awakened by the dogs licking and pawing her.

"Oh my God, stop it!" she squealed.

"Good morning. I take it you're not used to having animals around," observed Helmut wearily.

"No, I'm not. I'm really hungry. Mind if I poke around your kitchen and make some coffee?"

"I'd like some too. Go ahead and help yourself. I'm going to take a look at last night's pictures."

As Nina snooped around the kitchen, she came across a great deal of alcohol and mixers, top-of-the-line blenders, and espresso machines but no actual food.

"Looks like you could use a trip to the market," she said, handing him a steaming mug of espresso. "Do you shop at Rock 'n' Roll Ralph's on Sunset?"

"Oh, you mean Russian Ralphs. No, I have everything

delivered from Chalet Gourmet. So tell me about that tattoo on your shoulder. I noticed it last night."

"Ian and I got matching tattoos the night before we were married; it seemed like a good idea at the time, and I still love it."

"No regrets, huh? Good for you. Take a look at the pictures; I think we got some very cool shots." Nina studied the computer screen, amazed at how well they turned out.

"You have a real talent for taking sexy shots, Helmut. I'm guessing you've had a lot of practice," she said, curious about what else he had stored in his personal documents. "Anything else I can see? Open up the 'Blondes Don't Give a Damn' file."

"Sure, why not?" Helmut clicked open the document to reveal hundreds of photos he'd taken of, what else, tall, leggy blonde model types in various states of undress. Some were posed in black vinyl bras and boots clutching riding crops—very fetishy like his mannequins. Others were nude in black spiked heels, heavily made up, and expressionless, very Helmut Newton like. A few blondes were topless with cigarettes hanging from their lips wearing eyepatches.

"Wow, there is certainly no question about your preferred physical type. Where did you find so many women?"

"Some are friends, and I have girls sent over from a Hollywood Hills Hot Blonde Agency; they come by for about a hour or two. It's nothing serious, babe. It's for my own private collection," he said coolly.

"So, what's up with the eye patches?"

"Oh, that's for when I get in a … you know, *Kill Bill* kind of mood."

"I see. How intriguing. You really are quite a *unique collector*."

"What do you say we take a drive to Malibu and grab some lunch?" he said, his eyes glued to the computer screen. "We can stop at the Getty on the way back."

"I would love to, Helmut, but I don't have anything to wear. I mean, well, you know, besides last night's dress and the Lola's Lounge stuff," she stammered. "Honestly, I really need to get home and take a shower, relax, regroup. I've had a pretty stressful week."

"Yes, I guess you have. Another time then. Before I forget, I made something for you," he said, reaching into a drawer. "I thought you would like to have this. You can listen to it on the way home," he said, handing her the Ian Blackmoor Experience album on CD. "And don't forget your overnight bag next time."

"Helmut, thank you so much, I can't wait to hear this. And I want to thank you again for buying my paintings. I still can't believe it. I'll remake that 'Midnight Chloe' for you, and let me know when you want to do a Vegas run." She kissed him and walked swiftly out the door. Donning her new Lola's Lounge sunglasses, she eased back down Laurel canyon and popped in Ian's CD. She listened carefully to his vocals and lyrics like it was the very first time. Her mind swirled with memories of Ian and how wildly attracted they had once been. Would she ever experience that instant magnetism, that sexual chemistry and crazy, off-the-hook love again? Probably not. She'd hoped to find it with Helmut, but something didn't feel right. Something was missing. Should she try to contact Ian? As she contemplated the string of men who had come in and out of her life, she wondered what to do next. She decided that she would have to come clean with Tommy.

Two-Buck Chuck

Luxuriating in a long, hot bubble bath put Nina in a relaxed mood, which mentally prepared her to call Angie and Tommy. She flopped on the bed and called Angie first. "Hi, Angie, it's me. I'm sorry about last night."

"At last, the prodigal artist returns," she sniffed. "I guess you were too excited about your sellout show to be bothered to call me back."

"No, it's not like that. Give me a break, I really am sorry. Of course I'll be thrilled to get my Hard Edge check, but let's face it, if it wasn't for Helmut, I would have only sold one painting, and it's thanks to Brandon that I got in the show in the first place. The whole thing was kind of a fluke, really; it hardly qualifies me for hot, new, emerging female artist of the year."

"You can still register for unemployment; I know I'm going

to. So, tell me the truth, what really happened last night? Did you spend the night with Helmut?"

"Yes, I did," she confessed.

"How was it?"

"Very interesting. Kind of kinky."

"Are you in love with *him* now?"

"No, I'm not. I like Helmut. He's a fascinating man but I don't want to be an addition to his uhh … *blonde collection*. I didn't really feel like the chemistry was all there. I can't explain it right now."

"So, what are you going to do about Tommy?" she demanded.

"I'm going to call him next. I'm dreading it, but I have to talk to him. I'll let you know how it goes."

Nina was apprehensive about calling Tommy, so she turned on the news with the sound off and sunk deeper into the fluffy satin pillows for support before reaching for the phone.

"Hi, Tommy, it's me. I'm really sorry about last night."

"You didn't come home last night, did you?"

"No, I didn't. I wound up going to see Chiarra's show at the Lola's Lounge with Brandon and Helmut. You would have loved her act."

"Thanks, Nina, only I wasn't exactly invited. Just tell me the truth. Did you sleep with Helmut?" he asked angrily.

"Uhh … yes I did. Please don't get mad, Tommy. I'm really sorry."

"Yeah, well, sorry isn't good enough. I can't believe you could do this to me. I can't talk to you right now. Don't even think about calling me back. We're done." Click. He hung up, and just like that, it was over. Her playhouse crashed again.

Teary eyed, she contemplated her past. She had gone from Cote D'Azur glamour girl to almost-famous rock star wife, exotic dancer, B-actress, museum concierge, and playgirl artist. She had alternated high heels, bikinis, stripper gear, designer duds, suits and gowns, and burlesque club attire. What had become of the once-shy, artistic euro child? How many layers did she have to peel? Would she have to reinvent herself yet again?

Lying on the bed, completely exhausted, she turned up the volume of the COX 11 Eyewitness News, and there was Hunter Newman with an update on Helen's case.

"Internet dating gone wrong; reporting a breakthrough in the Helen Boyle case. A new suspect, forty-six-year-old Johnny Ramada, is currently being held in the Toro Beach jail as homicide officials continue the investigation. An anonymous tip was phoned in by a local dog walker who spotted Helen Boyle's bronze suburban in Ramada's garage. Officers searched the vehicle, discovering a small, unregistered pistol in the glove box. Also found was her laptop containing hundreds of online dating e-mails to the men registered with wellhungnready.com, to which Ramada had gold membership access. During questioning, he admitted to the knowledge of her accidental death, which apparently took place while showering after consuming three bottles of Charles Shaw red wine, also known as two-buck Chuck. This was, according to Ramada, preceded by a particularly strenuous bout of sexual activity. According to the suspect, there was no foul play. She slipped and hit her temple on the shower bar, and the blunt force caused the trauma to her head, Ramada said. He discovered her dead on the shower floor, he told police. Because of his prior run-ins with the law, he panicked and wrapped the body in the shower curtain with duct tape and disposed of it behind a Toro Beach pier dumpster, Ramada disclosed. The medical examiners, who will be taking DNA samples, and officials at the county coroner said they had no further information on the case at this time. I'm Hunter Newman with COX 11 News. Now back to you, Janey Bardot."

"Hi, ladies, a message for all of you online daters. Meet your men in public places, keep mace in your handbag, stay sober if possible, and shower at home. I'm Janey Bardot. Stay tuned for more Eyewitness News and Style File at nine o'clock."

What a way to go, thought Nina. She truly felt bad about ever toying with the idea of poisoning Helen and dialed Albert. "Hey, it's Nina, how are you? Have you seen the news?"

"Yes, I was just going to call you. I'm so relieved it's finally over."

"Did you know she owned a *gun?*"

"No, but right before she threw me out that night, she threatened to *blow my balls off* and make a eunuch out of me! Those were her last words to me, but I swear I had no idea she actually had a gun in the car," he stammered. "I just want to put it all behind me. I'm going to put the house on the market and move back to San Luis Obispo. What about you, Nina? What are your plans?"

"I don't know. I … really don't know. I'm just not sure. I need a new direction. I need to *break on through to the other side.* You know what I mean?"

"No, not really, but I'm sure you'll do well with whatever avenue you pursue. Thanks for sticking up for me. Let's keep in touch."

"Call me when you get settled, Albert. You can start a new chapter now too."

Nina was feeling alone and self-indulgent, and a wave of nostalgia washed over her as she reached for a white, leatherbound journal that she had been meaning to write in for a long time. As she stared at the blank book, she picked up a pen, and suddenly the words flowed easily. The black ink glided across the crisp white paper, filling each page with memories of her past. She wrote feverishly for hours, unable to stop until she heard the familiar foreign voice on the answer machine. It was Maximillian.

"Nina, please pick up. It is *very* important."

"Hello, Maximillian. How nice to hear from you. Is everything all right?"

"No, it's your *maman*. She is in the hospital with pneumonia; I think you should come to Paris at once."

"*Oh my God.* Of course, I'll come right away," she gasped.

"You may want to ask the museum for a leave of absence. She is very weak, and you may be gone a long time."

"It doesn't matter. I lost my job. I'll book a flight immediately. I'll start packing right now."

C'est La Vie

Nina's mother recovered over the summer with the help of Nina's devoted round-the-clock care in her apartment on Rue de Bourgogne on the Left Bank. Sadly, she had a relapse and passed away in the fall. Maximillian was there to assist with the arrangements and the services before returning to Vienna. Overcome with grief and feeling empty and abandoned, Nina rarely left the apartment. Still mourning, she finally forced herself out to explore the streets, wandering idly through cathedrals, museums, boutiques, and flea markets, rediscovering the beauty of Paris. One day while dining alone in one of her favorite bistros, she came to the realization that she was rapidly becoming unemployable and facing fifty. She knew it was time for a serious change. Meanwhile, her mother's inheritance and the sale of her Emerald Beach townhome had allowed for a certain insouciance, causing her to become somewhat ambitionless. She had lost her drive to paint, and with no friends and no men in her life or family left, she fell in love with the amazing French food. The endless bistros, boulangeries, patisseries, and chocalatiers lining the cobbled stone streets beckoned her with every delectable and tempting display. Having gained a few pounds, she resisted the urge to eat any more petit *gateau a chocolat.*

While savoring a café au lait at Café Belle Epoque near the Palais Royal one afternoon, she was engrossed in the parade of fashionably dressed French women, admiring their chic style. A slender, well-dressed man approached her, courteously introducing himself as Rene Clement, an aspiring French filmmaker. He was looking to cast the part of the mother of a hot new starlet he'd recently discovered for an upcoming low-budget production of *Les Aventures Erotiques de Juliette.* Apparently Nina had exactly the look he was seeking to play the girl's sexy mother. Not one to pass up such an unexpected opportunity and with her much-improved French, she auditioned and got the part. The film, much like the *Emmanuelle* series, became an underground hit in France and spawned two sequels, propelling Nina to low-budget art house erotic fame with a devoted cult following. She was relatively happy with her new life and independence, and she found that she was not particularly attracted to French men in general and adjusted to being single. Busy working and promoting her films, she had lost touch with her old friends in Emerald Beach over the past three years, with the exception of a postcard from Jack in Thailand. Naturally, she was more than delightfully surprised to receive an envelope postmarked from the States. She carefully opened the beautiful white-and-silver embossed card. It was, in fact, an invitation that read as follows:

Mr. and Mrs. Nguyen Kwan

and

Mr. and Mrs. Robert Collins

Request the Honor of Your Presence at the Marriage of

Angie Thuy Kwan to

Tommy Robert Collins Jr.

On Saturday the Fourteenth of April, 2007

At two o'clock in the afternoon at St. Catherine's Church

1009 Starling Way

Emerald Beach, CA

Angie and Tommy. Angie and Tommy. She kept repeating it over and over. She was stunned. Tommy was marrying Angie. How did it happen? She could only blame herself for losing Tommy. Angie had always been so concerned about him. Had Angie always secretly wanted Tommy? She was feeling somehow oddly betrayed, and she had to remind herself that three years had gone by. She had never made any effort to contact him. She finally snapped out of it, poured herself a glass of cabernet, and filled out the RSVP card. She made the necessary arrangements to fly to Emerald Beach.

***

As Nina unpacked her Louis Vuitton luggage in the Five Seasons Hotel suite, she selected a black cashmere sweater and a snug, camel-colored, knee-length skirt to wear for the day. She slid on a pair of black, patent-leather, high-heel Chanel pumps and swept up her long hair in an elegant chignon. With a wistful air, she fastened her Cartier watch that she bought for herself with her first Clement Productions film paycheck, braced herself, and called Angie.

"Hi, Angie, it's me. I'm here in Emerald Beach," she said, looking out the window at the once-familiar ocean view.

"Oh my God! Nina, I am *so* glad you could come. I've missed you so much; we are so excited to see you again."

"I've missed you too. I thought about you a lot and our good times at the EBC—well, you know, before everything crumbled. Can you believe it's been three years?" she asked, walking out of the hotel room.

"No, it is hard to believe. Nina, it's good to hear your voice again. You know, I have to tell you that I was really worried about how you would feel about me and Tommy being together and now *getting married.*"

"Honestly, Angie, I was completely stunned when I got the invitation. It took awhile for it to sink in, but I got over it and I, uhh, think it's wonderful. I'm very happy for both of you. But

I have to say that knowing you, I'm a little surprised you didn't plan a June wedding."

"Actually, that was the original plan, but we had to push up the date because I'm *pregnant!*"

"Wow, congratulations," Nina said, feeling a slight lump in her throat.

"Tommy and I are *so* excited to start a family. I'm teaching at Emerald Beach Middle School now, but I'll take maternity leave after summer vacation."

"Oh, Angie, that's great news." Nina paused to clear her throat. "I'm … very happy for you," she said, holding back a tear. "What about, Tommy?"

"Tommy's doing really well. Our parents helped buy the Barracuda Bar and turned it into an upscale sports bar. It's called the Hurricane Lounge now. Tommy manages it, and his dad helps out on the weekends."

"How nice for everyone," Nina said, trying not to come across too sardonic. "Sounds like everything worked out just perfect for both of you. Do you ever see or any of the old museum gang?"

"James is still there, and I heard that Rikki and Jessie's band got signed by a major label."

"That's great, good for them. I'll have to give the boys a call. I had a feeling that James would still be at the museum. What about Justine and Nadia?"

"I ran into them about a year ago. They're both at Long Beach University getting their MFAs. They got a postcard from Bangkok from Jack. I guess he's still in Thailand."

"I got one from him too. You know, I've always wanted to go there. Maybe I'll visit him this summer. What about Brandon?"

"He moved to New York and is working at MOMA. Apparently he has an erotic torso series that's selling really well. Speaking of erotic, we heard about your uhh … *French movies.*"

"Yes, well, I never dreamed *Juliette's Erotic Adventures* would be a success and that I would be such a big hit as her mom. The films do really well in Europe and Japan, but they probably won't make it to the States. They can't get any American distribution. Life is strange, isn't it? You never know what's around the corner. I can't wait to see you tomorrow. We have so much to talk about. It will be great to see Tommy again too. I've missed both of you. Who is coming? Anyone I know?"

"There will be a lot of people you know there, and everyone will be excited to see you again. You've been gone so long."

"Yes, it has been a long time. My life is so different in Paris. I'll tell you all about it. Let's try and catch up more at the wedding. You can give me a complete update. Right now I should probably turn my cell phone off."

"Why, what are you doing? Where are you going?"

"I'm about to walk into the EBC, Angie. I'll call you later. Bye."

She took a deep breath and hesitated before entering the museum. Memories flooded her brain as she stepped inside. It felt like a strange kind of homecoming after her three-year absence, which had changed the course of her life completely. She marveled at the museum's new look. Lacquered walls in a gleaming white finish soared easily sixty feet high with giant plasma screens flashing cutting-edge video art. A stunning new state-of-the-art, kidney-bean-shaped reception desk now replaced her old one. As she admired the renovation, her thoughts drifted back to that fateful spring of 2004, her final season at the EBC.